"Hamilton High is the setting for a new reality show, being shot as close to real-time as possible. Each week, everything that happens gets broadcast on Fox. You're going to be a TV star!"

Now, you might think that sounds like the most fabulous thing ever. I, Fiona O'Hara, don't. This was the first day of my Junior year, and I didn't want to be at Hamilton High in the first place. It filled me with a total sense of dread. Not just the normal feeling of dread that anyone feels when confronted with a brand-new school, teeming with strangers just waiting to turn one into social mincemeat. I had a deeper dread. A complex dread. A dread like no other that had ever hit Hamilton, New Jersey.

The kind of dread that accompanies the terms "high school" and "New Jersey" being used in one sentence.

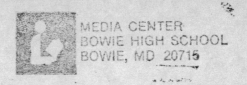

THE REAL DEAL
Focus on *THIS!*

Amy Kaye

smooch
New York City

SMOOCH®

November 2003

Published by

Dorchester Publishing Co., Inc.
200 Madison Avenue
New York, NY 10016

ISBN: 0-8439-5252-0

Printed in the United States of America.

For my mom, who's nothing like any
of the moms in this book;
For my dad, who's nothing like the dads;
And for my hometown, which is, in fact,
distressingly similar in every way.

THE REAL DEAL

Focus on *THIS!*

Prologue

I opened the door of the auditorium and was blinded by a thousand-watt halogen bulb.

"*Cut!*" someone yelled. "Who the hell is that?"

Bad, right? Then I heard something worse: the sound of two thousand high school kids laughing.

"Down in front!" someone yelled.

"Was that supposed to happen?"

Then a nonkid voice. Definitely grown-up—and angry: "Get her out of there, please."

I held my hand up, squinting and blinking like a laboratory rabbit getting a Reye's test. I couldn't move, because I couldn't see. Finally someone grabbed my arm and yanked me to the side.

"All right," my savior yelled. "You guys can start over." Then he—I knew it was a he, at least, because of the voice—turned to me and said, "Nice move. I thought they had the school in total lockdown?"

"This is my first day here," I explained. "I was supposed to show up first thing and report to the principal's office, but I didn't know where to catch my bus. So I had to walk. And I got lost. And by the time I got here, there wasn't anyone in the office. Is this Hamilton High School? What do you mean, lockdown?"

"Most of the show is shot without a script, but we're just doing the opening sequence now."

"Show? Opening sequence?" I was doing my rabbit imitation again. Also, I could see now, the guy who grabbed my arm was a dead ringer for Matthew McConaughey, without the annoying twang or bongo drums. In other words, gorgie. Which did not help me, Fiona O'Hara, in the keeping-my-cool department.

Fake-Matthew's face broke into the most dazzling grin I think I've ever seen. "Uh, yeah—the show. The opening sequence. Did you say you were *new* here?"

"Yeah. My mom just—"

"So you didn't know about the—"

"Show? Opening sequence? No, as you might be able to discern from the fact that I keep saying 'show' and 'opening sequence' like they're my mantra at yoga class. What is going on? Did I stumble onto a movie set?"

Fake-Matthew shook his head. "Oh, man. Yeah. See, they were supposed to tell everyone, and get the releases signed. Hamilton High—"

"Quiet on the set!" someone barked.

Matthew's voice dropped to a whisper, and he

stood very, very close to me, with a hand clamped around my upper arm in a, how you say, terribly intimate way. Which, combined with my frustration, confusion, and nervousness, caused me to flush bright pink when he finished his sentence:

"Hamilton High is the setting for a new reality show, being shot as close to real time as possible. Each week, everything that happens gets broadcast on Fox. You're going to be a TV star!"

You might think that sounds like the most fabulous thing ever. But I don't. This was the first day of my junior year, and I didn't want to be at Hamilton High in the first place. It filled me with a total sense of dread. Not just the normal feeling of dread that anyone feels when confronted with a brand-new school, teeming with strangers just waiting to turn one into social mincemeat. I had a deeper dread. A complex dread. A dread like no other that had ever hit Hamilton, New Jersey.

The kind of dread that accompanies the terms "high school" and "New Jersey" being used in one sentence, for instance.

Should I back up? I'll back up. I'm aware that

most adolescent girls in the sixteen- to eighteen-year-old range are afflicted with what you might call intense self-loathing and a general hatred of the circumstances of their lives. That, I have to say, is not me. Well, it *was* not me. I grew up in Manhattan, a small island off the East Coast that is, basically, the center of the universe. I went to Stuyvesant High School, an elite and competitive public school. I got good grades, I toed the line between popular and bookish, and I was so ahead of the game, I was about to be named the first nonsenior to head the school newspaper.

Then what happened? I'm not sure. My home life just exploded. See, my parents had never been the most solid pair. The sole purpose for my learning to talk, for instance, was apparently so I could referee their arguments. I'd be, like, five, and toddling back and forth between my dad, in the bedroom, and my mom, in the kitchen, as they complained about each other; somehow I learned to deliver the messages in such a way that they'd get over it before I starved to death.

That was fine for twelve years or so. But once I got to high school, I had bigger fish to fry. I mean, between the rigorous course schedule and my extracurriculars—plus my social life, which, I'm sorry, I think I'm entitled to have—I just didn't have time to worry about whether my dad was flirting with someone at work, or my mom was spending too much money, or who was not speaking to whom on the home front.

Before I knew it, our friendly, cluttered, homey little Upper West Side apartment had turned into a war zone. Overnight, it seemed, the deep freeze hit. The screaming arguments escalated. The flirting with other people got worse—on both sides. My parents started acting like two characters on a soap opera. And before I knew it, their marriage—and my world—had blown apart.

That was about a year and a half ago. That was when they set out on a campaign to get revenge on each other. For what? I don't know. They were just two people who'd never gotten along that well, had gotten married for unknown reasons, had stayed married because of me, and finally split up. But, man! They went after each other with a fury that would scare the spandex pants off of anybody in the World Wrestling Federation. With a speed previously unknown to humankind (or lawyers), they spent so much money lobbing briefs at each other, they had to sell our apartment just to keep from going bankrupt. Dad had to move in with friends. And Mom? Mom ran like a scared mouse far, far from the big city, back to the suburbs she grew up in.

We moved into my grandmother's basement. (My grandpa died when I was about ten. He was a sweet little guy, but kinda quiet.) In other words, we are now a bad stereotype.

My mom, now robbed of the daily routine of screaming at my dad and pretending to be an interior designer, completely fell apart. I begged her to figure out a way I could stay in the city for the rest of high school. I asked if I could live with Dad. Nothing doing: She'd gone the extra mile to get custody of me, and she wasn't about to give him the satisfaction of "getting me" after all that. (Thanks, Mom!) I tried to find a friend to take me in. Wonderful as they are, my friends live in apartments equally tiny. Besides, if my mom didn't have custody of me, she'd lose the monthly support payments that come directly from my dad's account, whether or not he has work as a television sound engineer. So off to Jersey I was dragged, kicking and screaming.

Literally. I actually kicked and I actually screamed.

Once we got here, Mom disintegrated into a miserable pile of flesh and Paxil. She had no idea where I should register for school. I had to do all that research myself. Grandma—Mom's mom—thought Hamilton High was just fine.

"I don't know why your parents felt the need to send you to that urban school in the first place," she sniffed. "I'm sure it was full of drugs and gangs."

Drugs and gangs. That's Grandma's assessment of anything that falls outside the borders of Hamilton Township. Meanwhile, Stuyvesant is a prep school and an automatic ticket to an Ivy League college. But Grandma doesn't know what those are, either. She knows Mr. Burns from *The Simpsons* went to Yale. That's about the extent of her experience with topnotch schools.

Don't get me wrong: I love my grandma. She and I always got along fine. But the way she and my mom relate to each other gives "dysfunctional" new meaning. Like I said, Grandpa died seven years ago, so it's just us three women living in this white clapboard house now. It's a fertile breeding ground for new and different styles of unhealthy interactions, let me tell you.

Anyway, that last week in Manhattan, while everyone else was escaping the August heat in Cape Cod or wherever, my principal let me use Stuyvesant's library to do some research. First, I found out Hamilton High was rated somewhere between average and middling in their academic standards. Then I discovered the local Catholic school was a repository for kids who got thrown out of the public school. Finally I tracked down Trenton Academy, a private school definitely in league with Stuyvesant. I called them. I begged them to take a look at my academic record. I faxed them my report cards and class projects. I even had my principal call their principal.

They weren't interested. Not only was I late, I was broke. No tuition, nothing doing. I was on my own and headed for Hamilton High. The chaos of my life left the administration of Trenton Academy unmoved, unsympathetic, and uncomfortable around me. People hate misfortune. They seem to think it's contagious.

And my friends? I could feel them subtly pulling themselves away. Divorce is one thing. But moving to New Jersey? A few miles across a river, but light-years away in terms of status. I was instantly tainted with its odor. I swear, my hair got slightly bigger without my doing a thing to it.

I'm exaggerating. Anyway, my best friend, Giuli, was up in Maine for the summer and wouldn't find out I was going until she got back for school. Becky, the third in our BF threesome, got really freaked out and just kind of flaked on me. She disappeared for a couple of days. Look, none of us had really been through anything bad before. We just rolled through life hitting sample sales for the best discounted designer duds, quizzing each other on calculus formulas, and keeping a running ironic and snide commentary on the world around us. It was an unspoken agreement: I wouldn't complain about my parents, Giuli wouldn't complain about her crackhead sister, and we'd all ignore Becky's eating disorder. Deep, authentic feelings were a mortal sin to us. So upon having them, I was sent here—to purgatory.

So here I was. Hamilton High. And now, it seemed, I had an even bigger surprise. Not only was my new high school full of strangers, it was also the location for a new reality series. If the producers took an interest in me, my every emotional meltdown, awkward moment, and bad zit (like there are good ones) would be fodder for a national audience.

I just hoped I could stay out of the way of the cameras. Thank goodness, the school had over two thousand students. How hard could that be?

I was about to find out.

chapter
one

"Sorry," I said. "'Scuse me. Can I . . . ? Thanks."

I sank gratefully into the first empty chair in my French class. It was bad enough I didn't know a soul. But they all seemed to know me. I wasn't just the new kid in school—I was also the doofus who'd stumbled into the auditorium in the middle of taping. The friendly smiles I sent out were returned with smirks, or averted gazes, or nothing at all. It was the most awful feeling.

Next to me was a girl with blond hair. I mean, the shade of blond that won you big points in the Third Reich. Also the shade of blond that you get from using Sun-In. She had it styled like it was a little yellow helmet on her head. Everything about her screamed "Sunday matinee." You know: the tourists who come into town in their acid-washed jeans and puffy white coats to see the understudy cast of *Rent* and buy souvenirs at Planet Hollywood. People from the Gray Line tours. Trust me, they're a species all their own. It was all I could do to keep myself from staring.

Sunday Matinee leaned over to me.

"Excuse me," she said.

"Yes?" I turned to her and gave her my sunniest grin. Hey, she might look like a tourist, but if she was going to be nice to me, this beggar wasn't about to be a fancy chooser.

"What is the deal with your outfit?" she asked, staring up at me with cornflower-blue eyes. Behind her, I heard a loud titter, I assumed from her best friend forever since second grade.

"What do you mean?" I asked, my polite smile frozen on my face.

"I mean, *what* are you wearing? Did you come here from a funeral or something?"

I looked down. I was wearing my favorite comfortable but presentable outfit: a Prada blazer from a sample sale, black tank, and tailored black slacks from Barney's.

"I don't know," I said. "Did you just come here from Wal-Mart?"

Ugh, I know. Way to make friends on the first day, Fiona. But you know what? I've never been smart about keeping my mouth shut. Especially when I'm being confronted by a girl in an oversize orange sweatshirt from the Gap paired with stretch jeans and white Reeboks. I mean, there is a limit to what I can take.

Sunday Matinee didn't even flinch. She just smiled broadly, indicating that I hadn't even dented her armor, and turned back to her friends, making loud and obvious whispery comments about me.

"Shut up, Judy. At least she doesn't look like she was cast from a mold at the conformist factory," a voice from behind me said. I couldn't resist: I had to look. The voice came from a strikingly pretty girl with a tumble of black curls springing out from her head, and a pale, almost Goth complexion. She was dressed in a low-level alternachick style: plaid skirt, black tights, Doc Martens, black t-shirt, and eyebrows plucked into neat, high arches. I tried to smile at her, but she avoided my gaze.

Judy didn't even turn around. "Whatever, freak," she said. "Now there's two of you."

Oh. I get it. "Freak" wanted to be nice, but didn't want to be allied with the new geek, in case I just made her life worse. Jeez. High school politics are mind-boggling.

Thank goodness, the teacher came in at that point, and we could all worry more about new textbooks than about who hated me the most. The only snag I hit was when the teacher, Mrs. Cohen, asked me a question in rapid French, and I answered with a flawless accent. Apparently that's not acceptable. Behind me I heard several snickers and a couple of throat-clearing approximations that sounded more like

Hebrew than the language of Molière. It seemed I was expected to play stupid in order to survive.

I noticed a little camera mounted in the upper right corner of the classroom, blinking and buzzing at regular intervals. I also spied some camera guys wandering around the hallways. The classroom doors were being kept open, I guess so they could come in and take a peek at us students whenever they felt like it. It was really distracting. I wondered why in the hell the school had agreed to such a ridiculous idea.

At the end of class, I noticed Freak dawdling, so I made my move.

"Hey, thanks," I said. "My name's Fiona. Fiona O'Hara. I'm new here, obvie."

"Yeah. I'm Claire," she said. "Good luck."

And that was the end of the dawdling. She took off like a shot. No invitation to eat lunch with her, no advice on how to handle Judy the Helmet. God! This place was tougher than the science fair.

I headed over to my English class and plopped into the first seat I saw open. I didn't even try to look around. This was totally demoralizing. I barely even noticed when a completely gorgeous guy—my second one of the day, but at least this one was my age—sat down next to me.

Uh-oh. He seemed to be looking at me. Still smarting from my earlier encounter with a local, I sank down in my seat, trying to look small. The last thing I needed was another—

"I hear you're a troublemaker."

I shifted my eyes to the left, trying to see who he was talking to. All I saw was a cardboard cutout of Zora Neale Hurston. So I shifted them back to the right.

Hellooo, sailor!

I beheld the brownest eyes the world has ever seen. They were like two gingersnaps floating in a glass of gorgeous milk. Um, that's a gross analogy, I know. But I was kind of knocked off balance by just how cute this guy was. Think Freddie Prinze Jr., only with olive skin and longer hair. And without the vampire-slaying wife, of course. He looked like a puppy dog with six-pack abs. I was flabbergasted.

"Wuh?" I said.

Brilliant, right?

Cutie-pie leaned in closer, grinning like the cat that ate the canary. "It's all over school, how Judy Kreiger tried to give you the usual treatment. And how you made a crack about her dad working at Wal-Mart. I'm telling you, that's never happened before."

"I didn't say her dad worked at Wal-Mart. I said she *shopped* there. Either way, it wasn't that good a comeback."

"Doesn't matter!" Cutie shook his head. "People just like to see her get slammed, no matter how it happened. I think you might be a legend."

I laughed. "Ohmigod, this is like a game of telephone. That was an absolute nonevent."

"We'll see." He nodded his head at me. "I'm Joey Maynard. And you're the new girl."

I shook his hand, grateful for the human contact. And such fine-looking human contact it was!

"Fiona O'Hara," I told him. "Guilty as charged."

Joey leaned back in his chair, his legs stretched out in front of him like he owned the place.

"I think this is going to be interesting," he said.

Indeed. Indeed, it was.

"Mom! Mom?" I called out when I got home.

"In here," my mom answered, in her now-usual tone of utter misery.

"Ma, I wanted to— Ugh."

My mom was in the finished basement we now shared, which was still decorated with her high school posters (Patti Smith, the Ramones, Iggy Pop—once upon a time, my mom was cool). She was lying flat on her back, staring at the ceiling, hugging a huge book to her chest.

"Mom?" I asked.

"I found this photo album," she said.

"Mom."

The photo album was a much-detested item around our old apartment. My parents, when they got engaged, wanted to get married at CBGB's, a punk club in downtown New York. But my grandparents insisted on a dorky wedding at the Hamilton Country Club. My young, pre-me parents went along with it just to keep the peace. Grandma created a fairy-tale wedding for her only daughter (I think that must have been the one day in my life, besides the day she was born and was swaddled in hospital blankets, that my mother wore white). And she documented it all in the ultimate over-the-top wedding photo album, complete with white leather binding, dangling ribbons, and gold detailing, which she presented to my parents like it was the Holy Grail.

You don't understand. My mom *hates* this photo album. She *always* hated it. And now she was clutching it like it was a lifesaver from the *Titanic*.

"Look at me!" she demanded, sitting up and flipping it open. Her dyed-black bangs fell limply across her forehead and she brushed them aside impatiently. "Look. Look at how hopeful I looked. And your father. It's like he doesn't even want to be there."

"He *didn't* want to be there," I tried to point out. "Neither did you. There was a swan ice sculpture, for God's sake. You don't look hopeful! You look stoned! Because you were!"

"I thought getting married would make everything all right," she wailed. "Where did I go wrong? What did I do?"

"Mom."

"I'm a good person! I pay my taxes. I help old people!"

"No, you don't."

"Well, I will! If I can just feel better, if something good will just happen to me—"

"Mom, come on. Can we—"

"Oh, forget it," she moaned, rolling onto her stomach and burying her face in a pillow. "You have your whole life ahead of you; you could never understand."

I sighed, sat down next to her on the bed, and patted her heaving back.

"I'm going to have his ass on a platter."

Oh, no, I thought. *Not again.* I'd been hearing about the good old platter of ass since the divorce first broke. That's what she used to scream at my dad: "Go ahead! Leave me! I'll have your ass on a platter!" What a metaphor. It sounded unappetizing the first time I heard it—especially since the fancily presented ass in question was my dad's—and it didn't improve with age.

"Really, maybe it's time to—"

"Don't preach at me! You're worse than my mother!" She winged a pillow at me. It was extra soft, but yowch. I backed out the door and up the stairs—where I collided with the mother in question, my grandmother.

"Still sulking?" she asked, pursing her lips.

Like I said, my grandma and I have had some fun times together, like when I took her to the Westminster Dog Show. But she and my mom make oil and water look friendly. And I have this weird thing where I tend to want to protect my mom from her. Silly, I know, given that my mother had just hit me with the worst insult she could think of, plus a pillow. But Grandma, well-meaning as she is, tends to try to run her life. A job that Mom would prefer that *I* do.

It's complicated.

"She's okay," I assured her.

"Hmph. How was school?"

"Oh. Okay." I shrugged.

"Just as good as those fancy city schools, I'm sure," Grandma said. "And without the drug dealers and Crips."

"Grandma, there's no Crips at Stuyvesant."

"So you say." She turned on her heel and went into the living room to catch *Judge Judy*. I sat in the kitchen.

"Helloooo!" a cheerful voice called in from the back door. I was about to get up and open it when it swung open on its own. Grandma never bothered locking it—no matter how much I asked her to. She got insulted, like I was implying she lived in a bad neighborhood. And now we were about to be murdered in our own home by—

A lady carrying a casserole dish.

"Hello?" I said.

"Oh, hiiii!" she said, melting into a little heap of treacle. "You must be Fiona! Oh! Gosh! You're just the picture of your mother in high school! Except you don't wear all that pale makeup. Whoo! She really was different." The lady let loose a high-pitched titter, and I gritted my teeth.

"Different. Yeah," I said. "Can I help you with something?"

"Fiona! Don't be rude," Grandma said, breezing into the kitchen and hugging this stranger like she was the daughter she'd never had, then taking the casserole from her.

"This is Mary Dolan," she told me. "She and your mother were best friends growing up."

"Well, till high school," Mary Dolan piped up, turning her perkiness up to turbodrive. "Dunno what happened then, but we just sorta drifted apart. Kept in touch with your ol' grandma, though."

"And thank goodness. Mary's a wonderful person. A great help to me," Grandma said.

I could see she genuinely cared about this lady, but for the life of me, I couldn't see why. I sized her up in about three seconds, and that was probably a second longer than I needed. She was a complete and utter nerdball. She was wearing—I kid you not—stirrup pants, with an orange sweater and matching orange socks. Only the socks were decorated with a falling-leaves motif, to celebrate autumn, I suppose. I am serious. She had no idea what a fashion victim she was.

"Sorry I haven't come by before," she said. "I

know you got here at the end of August, but I just opened up a new store, and it's been total craziness."

"Mary is selling home accents and housewares," Grandma added.

"Yep-pers, I am, plus some gifts and things, candles and whatnot," Mary added. "A couple items for the ladies. Scented soap. You know."

Oh, I know, Mary. I know. I could just see the place: flowery curtains, lavender everything, and more of those themed socks.

Mom thumped up the stairs from the basement and shoved the door open.

"Can you make me coffee?" she asked me.

"Um, Mom, there's a—"

"Heeeyyyy!" Mary shrieked.

Mom gave her one look and slammed the door. We could hear her thumping back down.

"Oh, Mary, I'm sorry," Grandma said.

"Well, that sure brings back memories!" Mary said, her perky voice never changing. "Well, I'll be sure to come by again. I know how she feels. Maybe she'll be in a better mood next time."

Mary left, and I closed the door behind her. I knew better than to let on to Grandma how awful I thought my mom's supposed old friend was. But I had to ask.

"Grandma, what did she mean, she knows how Mom feels?"

"She's newly single too," Grandma said. "Saddest thing. Her husband broke up with her because she couldn't have children. They tried for years to get pregnant and never could, so he went and found someone else. She's big as a house now, the new wife—twins. And poor Mary's on her own, trying to make a living for the first time."

"Oh, ugh!" I said, suddenly feeling bad for her.

This whole place was tainted, it seemed. Grandma left the kitchen and I stared at the wooden table. Nothing good could happen here. Cameras followed me around all day, and perky tragic women turned up at home. All I wanted was to run back to our little place in the city, where things were safe, I knew my enemies—and I used to have friends.

It was going to be a long year.

chapter TWO

Did I say a long year? The first week lasted about a century. I almost starved to death. There's nothing worse than sitting alone in a school cafeteria, so I spent lunch hour in the library, thumbing through the eight books in their collection.

I exaggerate. There had to be at least twelve. It was like death by Jacqueline Susann.

The only bright part was Joey. He didn't have the same lunch period as me, but at least I saw him in English. He and I moved to the back of the class and cracked jokes the whole time. It wasn't like I needed to pay much attention anyway. We were reading Hemingway, *A Farewell to Arms*, which I read over the summer like two years ago. Most of the class consisted of reading each chapter out loud and then taking a quiz on what we'd just read.

Joey was much more interesting.

"Where did you move here from?" he asked me.

"New York City," I said.

"What part?"

"Upper West Side" I said.

He nodded like he knew it. Then he cracked up and shook his head. "I have no idea where that is," he admitted.

"I don't get it," I said in a hiss, as we dodged

dirty looks from Mrs. Lewinson. "How do you live within spitting distance of the city and never go there?"

"My parents are scared of it," he whispered back. "We used to go in about once a year to get some enforced culture. But the last time we went was like three years ago."

"What went wrong?"

Joey's eyes flickered to the floor and he kind of blushed. "On our way to the Lincoln Tunnel, we passed a hooker," he said.

"Oh, you're kidding."

He started to laugh with this hissing sound that was totally adorable. "I'm serious. And it was one of those ones with her shirt off."

"Oh, no!" I snickered. "I know what you mean. It freaked out your parents, huh? Jeez, they're lucky she only took off her shirt."

"What do you mean?"

"For a while, there was a little bit of a problem with the transvestites in that area," I told him. "The real females and the fake ones were having a bit of a turf war. So the real girls started displaying that they had . . . the necessary goods."

Joey turned bright red and put his head down on his desk, completely unable to speak, he was laughing so hard. "What do you mean? They didn't wear—"

"It's true," I told him. "You'd drive past them and think you just went through Sherwood Forest."

Joey dissolved into hysteria, tears streaming out of his eyes. I was trying to keep him quiet, but Mrs. Lewinson stood up and glared at us. Then she put one manicured finger on the desk of the girl who was reading, signifying that she should stop. The class fell silent.

"Joseph," she said in a sharp voice.

"Sorry!" he hooted, his face buried in his arms.

"Miss O'Hara." She spat my name out like it tasted bad. "Perhaps you'd like to tell us what's so funny."

"We were just talking about Robin Hood," I said.

She gave me a look of intense displeasure. Heads turned toward me like periscopes in an ocean of embarrassment. My face burned, but somehow it wasn't so terrible. Because Joey was in it with me. We were bad kids!

"Sorry," I peeped.

"Snck," Joey snorted.

Mrs. Lewinson moved Joey to the other side of the classroom and we spent the rest of the class period studiously avoiding looking at each other, desperate to avoid another giggle fit. I didn't want to get sent to the principal's office.

Okay, so maybe the week wasn't a complete waste.

There was another bright spot. Pete Steinway. I thought Pete was just a cute buddy for me to pass some time with. Little did I know, later, he would turn out to be my total and complete saving grace.

I was coming around the corner, heading for the gym, when I saw a couple of big football players. They were clearly up to something. I could only see their backs, but they seemed to be ganging up on someone. Someone small.

As I got closer, I assessed the situation. I determined that one of them was lean and wiry, with a stylized oval of facial hair covering his chin. The other was more muscular—I guess you could call him buff. And they both looked like bad news.

I was planning to walk past with my head down. I figured, the school's dotted with cameras, right? Nobody's going to let this happen in this day and age.

I glanced up. No cameras in this corner of the

school. These two meatheads were actually crafty enough to find a spot where they wouldn't be captured on film. Of course, there were no roving cameramen, either. Just me. Me. The new girl.

"Why don't you guys just let me go," I heard a quavery, brave voice say. Sure enough, these two geniuses were confronting a threatening creature who was about the size of a drinking straw. He was thin, with a shock of pale blond hair, and he was wearing chinos with a neat, cute blue Quiksilver sweater. Oh, man. He was dead meat.

"Oh, we'll let you go," Chin Hair said. "But we're going to take your pants first."

Chin Hair's beefy friend didn't say a word, for or against. He just folded his arms. I was hit by a wave of angry heat just listening to this. And so Bigmouth (that's me) struck again.

"Isn't that a little *gay*?" I asked.

Chin Hair stopped and turned his head to look at me. His hands were still on the shoulders of the little fella. But his attention was all mine. I looked straight into his dead-looking eyes and stared him down.

"I mean, you're asking for the guy's *pants*," I said. "That's so homoerotic. That's really brave of you to come out like that."

"I'm not! He is!" Hairy Chin said, shoving the kid backward like he'd just been burned.

"Hey, it's no big deal," I said. "I mean, isn't that why you're on the football team? So you can hang out with a bunch of other guys, shower together, roll around on the field together, basically share the all-male love?"

"Just keep walking," he told me.

"Sure. But he's coming with me."

"Oh, man. Forget it. Come on, Baxter."

Beefy Baxter looked like he didn't know what to do or say. In other words, *durr.* It gave me complete and total satisfaction to watch him follow his dumb friend down the hallway, back to whatever cave they had crawled out of. I turned to the kid.

"Does that happen a lot?" I asked him.

"Oh . . . every once in a while," he said, readjusting the collar of his shirt so it fell neatly under his sweater.

"I hope you don't mind—"

"No! No, of course not," he said, patting down his pants to straighten the pleat.

"I can't believe being gay still matters out here."

"Hey, how about you don't make the same assumption they did?" he snapped, with a sharpness that was like a slap in the face.

"Ouch!" I said. "I was just saying—"

"I know what you were saying—"

"Hey! Hey," I said, grabbing his upper arm. He was wired to the gills on fear, adrenaline, and anger. I could feel it like an electrical pulse. "Hey. Whatever. I don't care, you know? I'm not . . . I'll leave you alone."

I turned to go, but he stopped me.

"I'm sorry," he said. "It's just . . . people have been calling me a fag since I was five. It's like I never had a say in it. I mean, yeah, I'm gay. But I'd rather be Pete than Gay Pete. I just don't want to broadcast it. Maybe I'm just not ready for everybody to . . . "

His voice trailed off. I took his hand and squeezed it. Oh, my God. Poor guy. "Like I said, I don't care," I told him. "Honestly."

"Pete Steinway," he said, turning our hand-squeeze into a handshake.

"Fiona O'Hara," I told him. "I'm new here."

"Yeah, no kidding." He laughed sheepishly. "Thanks a lot for that. It's not every day you get rescued by a girl."

"Oh, you would've been fine. I just felt like telling off some gorillas."

"Well, you did a bang-up job. Where you headed?"

"Gym. I got here too late to sign up for anything, so I have to do weight training."

"Oh, me too," Pete said. "I missed signup day to go into the city for the *American Idol* auditions."

"You're kidding." I shook my head. "Who needs *American Idol* when you've got cameras all over the school?"

"Ah, they'll never notice me here." He waved me off. "Anyway, I like to cover all my bases."

"So how'd you do?"

"Um . . . I did fine, which is bad. I wasn't good enough to get picked, and I wasn't bad enough to be on the rejects reel. So they didn't notice me, either."

"I think most people would say that's good," I pointed out.

"I guess. So anyway, that was some slap-fight you got into with Judy, huh?"

I groaned as we walked down the hall together. "This gets bigger and bigger every time I hear about it," I complained. "Now it's a slap-fight. Next thing you know they'll be saying I bit off her ear and sent it to Mike Tyson."

"Now, that'd be news." Pete laughed.

"Seriously, you think you're going to get something out of this reality show?" I asked.

"I dunno. It worked for. . . um."

"Yeah, see, I don't think it works for anyone."

"Well, Colleen from *Survivor* was in that Rob Schneider movie," he pointed out.

"Uh, yeah . . . "

"And Judd from *The Real World* writes for Batman comics."

"That's *very* famous."

"I dunno." Pete shrugged. "It's the American way, right? Get your fifteen minutes of fame any way you can."

"I guess. What I can't figure out is why the school's letting them do it," I complained. "It's so distracting."

"Oh, that's easy. We had this totally corrupt mayor, and the school district ran out of money before he was incarcerated. The state didn't have any to give us, so the school district made a deal with the devil. Or the network, anyway."

"You're kidding." I shook my head. "For the money. And you guys are the sacrificial lambs?"

"Baaa," Pete said.

When I came out of gym, fully pumped up from my session on the Nautilus machine, I headed straight up to the library. Pete had the same lunch period as me—great news! I might actually get to eat some frozen pizza before homecoming!—but he had some kind of detention thingie from when he cut school for the big audition. So I'd have to visit my old haunt one last time.

Good thing, it turns out.

I was wandering up and down the aisles between the shelves, breathing in that very particular smell that libraries have. You know, that papery-plasticky book smell? I don't know, I had nothing better to do. The librarian kept giving me the hairy eyeball. She wasn't used to students coming here of their own accord.

I noticed a couple of books were out of place, so I started alphabetizing them. I pulled *Pa-Ph* out and saw a face staring at me from behind them. I stifled a little scream, then laughed.

"Joey," I said. "What are you doing here?"

"I heard you spent lunchtime here," he said. "I thought I'd see what the big draw was."

"Very elite lunch spot," I told him. "Only the coolest of the cool know about it. All the supermodels love it."

"What's the menu like?"

"That's why the supermodels love it," I revealed. "It's the only lunch spot in town that doesn't serve any food."

"Aaah." Joey nodded.

He came around to my side of the bookshelf. We were totally secluded. I took half a step back because he was so close. Not that it was bad. It was just . . .

I could feel the heat of him through his shirt. I looked up and met his eyes. His breath was warm. His lips were inches away from mine. I tilted my head back just a bit, to challenge him.

"What are you doing here?" I asked again.

"I wanted to check something out," he said, his eyes flickering from my eyes to my lips and back up again.

"A book?"

"Yeah, a book. Or something I can read like one."

I leaned back against the back wall. There was no place else to go. Not that I wanted to be anyplace else. This was the best thing that had happened to me since we'd returned the U-Haul.

"Oh, very clever," I purred. "Think you can read me like a book, huh?"

"Not really." Joey shook his head. "Actually, I've got no idea what's going on in here." He tapped my forehead lightly with a finger. "I can't stop thinking about you."

"I must be a bestseller."

He shook his head. "Why don't you drop the armor?" he asked.

I shrugged. "No armor," I said. "This is just me."

"It's going to take some getting used to."

I felt like my knees were going to ooze into my shoes. Was he going to kiss me? Was he saying he wanted to be my boyfriend? You've got to remember, the guys I went to Stuyvesant with I'd known forever. There weren't a lot of surprises. And we were all so studiously blasé about everything. But Joey was so intense. I felt like we were repeating dialogue out of *Dawson's Creek*. The late-night version.

"Who says I want you to get used to—"

My clever line was interrupted by a tongue, two lips, and the gentle-rough clicking of teeth against teeth. Uhhh. Time stretched out like salt-water taffy as Joey and I kissed.

At first it was a hard kiss, like he was afraid if he didn't come at me full-force, I'd run away. But I didn't run away. So when it was clear I was returning his kiss, he pulled back slightly, rubbing his lips against mine and flicking his tongue gently around mine. I opened my eyes slightly, not to look back at him, but just to get a sense of how close he was to me. To check if this was really happening. Through the small blurred space between my eyelashes, I saw his arm leaned against the wall next to my head, the button of his jeans glinting brightly. I carefully brought my hands up to put them on his shoulders, just where they met his chest. Muscles. Long, lean muscles.

He gave a soft groan, like he felt welcomed, and put a hand on my waist. I thought I'd die of that. My entire body felt like a geyser of heat.

Finally he pulled back and looked down at me. He had a sly smile on his face. I felt like I was beaming like an idiot.

"Okay," I said. It was all I could think of!

"Very nice," he said.

The bell rang. Lunch was over. But I was positively ravenous—for more Joey.

"How about we meet up after school?" he asked. "I could drive you home."

"Sure," I said. "I hate the bus."

"See you later, then," he whispered. "Under the big tree out front." Then he kissed my cheek (how cute is that?) and strolled out of the library like the coolest guy on the planet.

Maybe this was shaping up, after all.

Or maybe not. Maybe not at all. Because when classes ended, I waited under the giant tree at the front of the school, where he'd told me to wait. Like a giant idiot, I waited. And waited. And *waited*. Need I tell you, no Joey?

I felt like a total and complete jerk. I didn't know who to be mad at: him, or me for believing he'd show. As I stood there under that great white oak or whatever it was, looking at the cookie-cutter wood-frame houses across the street, eyeballing each car that slowed as it passed me and then sped up, watching people get on their buses and disappear as the place got emptier and emptier and emptier until I was left standing there utterly alone . . . I just wanted to shrivel up and die.

Let's look at the facts: A year ago I was at the top of my game. Great school, reliable friends, incredible teachers. Okay, so my home life wasn't the best, but who noticed? And here I was now—stuck at this school where people made fun of you for having a real French accent. My old friends totally moving on with their lives, forgetting about me. Waiting for a guy to pick me up, and with no other way to get home, now that my bus had left.

I was ready to break down and cry. Except there just didn't seem to be any tears. All I could think was: He said he'd take me home, and he just didn't show. How rude is that? *What's wrong with me*?

A car finally pulled up. It was sporty-looking. I'd tell you what kind it was, but I have no idea. I'm a proud MetroCard-carrying member of the subway masses. In fact, I don't understand this whole suburban obsession with cars.

Or I didn't—until I found myself stranded without one in a world without subways.

I peered over at the car. That had to be Joey, right? But I didn't want to run over and look stupid. The driver's-side door opened. And guess who stepped out?

It wasn't Joey.

It was Not-Matthew. The cute grown-up from my little run-in with the spotlight.

I strolled forward as he leaned against the front fender and grinned at me.

"Just what is so funny?" I asked.

He shook his head. "Man, you really are a character," he said.

"What are you talking about?"

Without answering, he introduced himself. "I'm Mike. Mike Millman. The assistant director of this TV show we're filming here."

"Oh. Right," I said, turning around to look at

the school. "The people responsible for buying out the integrity of this educational institution and distracting the entire student body." I turned back to him. "Ever hear of the separation of church and state?"

"Last time I checked, network TV wasn't a religion."

"Shows what you know." I leaned against the fender, next to him. "So you're out here from the city."

"Yep. And so are you, I gather."

I nodded. "I just want to go back. Where do you live?"

"Sixth Street and Second Avenue."

"Uch! The East Village!" I sighed. "Rich hipsters living in overpriced tenements. God, I miss it!"

"What happened?"

"Long story. Bad divorce, depressed parents."

"You couldn't stay with friends through the end of high school?"

I shook my head. "No room. Manhattan's a tiny island, you know. And anyway . . . " I sighed. "I thought my place was with my mother. Now I'm not so sure."

"So what happened this afternoon?" he asked.

I shrugged. "I got blasted by the kissing bandit," I said. "Maybe his car broke down or something."

"Let me give you a ride home," Mike Millman said. "It'll all become clear in the end."

I shot him a sharp look. "What's that supposed to mean, Mr. Cryptic?"

He shrugged. "It means don't sweat it. You're going to be a star. A few days from now you won't have to worry about spending lunchtime in the library."

I got into the passenger side of his car, careful to keep my cell phone in hand, both to bonk him with and to call 911 if something weird happened.

But nothing did. The totally hot Mike Millman just drove me home, once I figured out where that was, and he was very charming and cool to boot. Too bad he's ten years older than me, I thought as I stepped out of his stick-shifting chariot.

I leaned down, propping myself up on his open window.

"Well, thanks for the ride," I said.

"No, thank *you*," he told me.

"For what?"

"You'll see." He chuckled, then drove off.

"What is with that?" I asked nobody in particular as I stood on the sidewalk in front of my grandparents' house. I kept muttering as I went up the walk. "Mr. Mysterious. The hell? Say what you mean."

"Talking to yourself, first sign of insanity," Grandma said as she passed me walking in the front door.

"I thought the first sign was speaking in sentence fragments," I muttered.

"Your father called," she sang, knowing it'd stop me in my tracks.

"What'd he say?" I asked.

"You can't go see him this weekend," she said. "He's moving again and there's no place for you. Couch surfing, he called it. Said you should talk to your mother about how much child support she's asking for, if you had a problem with it."

If my heart didn't feel like a lump of coal already, it did after that. My big weekend in the city: gone. And I was nothing but a joker in my parents' game of five-card stud. Fine.

When I got inside, the phone was ringing. I let it ring, but whoever it was hung up on the answering machine and called again. And again. Fine!

"Hello," I grunted.

"Is that Fiona?"

"Who is this?"

"It's Pete Steinway, you dink. Who else is going to be calling you?"

Who, indeed. Not my dad, not Giuli or Becky, and certainly not Joey.

"What is up, my weight-lifting friend?" I asked. Despite everything, there was something about Pete that didn't let me stay sad. Maybe it was the fact that his voice was so friendly. Or maybe it was just the fact that *any* voice was friendly—to me.

"Well, so? Are you going to watch?"

"Watch what?"

"Watch what!" Pete shrieked. "Duh, it's only the world premiere of Hamilton High on national network television tonight."

"What? I thought they taped for six months and then put the shows together. That's how it works with *The Real World*."

"Well, not this show. That's their whole hook. They want to see people in the school *react* to the show being on TV *as it happens*."

"Do you always speak in italics?"

"So are you going to come over tonight?"

"Oh. I don't know."

"Fiooonaaa?" My mom's voice quavered up the stairs toward me, like trails of stinky Limburger cheese in a Bugs Bunny cartoon. "Are you home? Can you bring me a pint of Ben & Jerry's from the freezer?"

"I'll be there," I said to Pete. "What time?"

"Eight P.M. Eastern, seven Central and Mountain."

"And uh . . . how do I get to your house?"

"Just look out your window." I lifted the cheery flowered curtains to see Pete peering back at me through his kitchen window, across the backyard.

"Oh!" I said, waving at him. "Okay. I'll see you at seven-fifty-seven."

"Bring Doritos." He hung up.

I went to the freezer and got the Ben & Jerry's. It'd keep my mom quiet long enough for me to get my homework done. Then I'd go take a look at this freakshow. See if I knew anyone who made it to the screen. What the hell, it would make a good story for when I moved back to the city. Which I'd do as soon as my dad found a big enough apartment.

Little did I know.

THE REAL DEAL: Episode One

Review in the Daily Post

Newest Nadir in Reality TV: The hit hits the fans as Hamilton High strikes a stunning debut.

For those of you who thought Survivor *was groundbreaking, prepare yourselves. Because in the hottest new television series pit stop, the tropical island riddled with poisonous snakes, cursed with inadequate food supplies, and crawling with cameramen is replaced by a truly terrifying locale: an average New Jersey high school.*

In an added twist, the show is shot as close to realtime as possible. How they do it is a mystery, but the producers throw together footage from the week for each Friday's episode. Thus, viewers will get to witness the students' reactions to seeing themselves the week before.

It's sick. It's twisted. And it's already a ratings winner.

The first episode opens with a bang: A new student, identified only as Fiona, stumbles into the auditorium during an assembly and causes a total scene. Oh, the humiliation! It's hard to watch—but harder to tear oneself away.

Throughout the hour, we see the willowy, fashionable Fiona attempting to worm her way into the rigid social structure of the local lunkheads. It's not easy. She humiliates the queen bee, one Judy, who falls from her throne as a result of Fiona's sharp-tongued verbal sparring. And the whole school is immediately abuzz.

Plot B focuses on Claire Marangello, a raven-haired beauty with porcelain skin and tumbling curls, madly in love with her longtime boyfriend, Joey. We see them tongue-wrestling under the bleachers, behind the auditorium, inside the phone booth at the school's main entrance. They seem to have no shame. But as Claire peers up at Joey with naked doe-eyed admiration, we learn something she doesn't know: Fiona has set her sights on him.

And gets him, too. At the end of the episode, a camera captures the new girl putting the moves on Claire's Joey in the library. We can't hear what's being said—the camera is shooting through the window, with a paparazzi-style zoom lens—but the hot-and-heavy smoochfest is hard to misinterpret. The producers of the show are either to be commended or arrested.

The show ends with a lingering shot of Fiona as she waits for Joey to pick her up after school.

And what will happen now? Far be it from this reviewer to make predictions, but it seems likely that no one will be able to resist finding out. And much as it shames me to admit it, I'll be right there, watching it along with the rest of America.

chapter THREE

I refused. I absolutely refused to go to school on Monday. I was going to get eaten alive!

"*No*!" I shouted when my grandma came into the basement bedroom.

"You're going to school," she said.

"I'm *not*. I want to go back to the city. I want my dad. I hate this place. I can't go back to that school."

"Everybody feels that way," my grandma insisted.

"Grandma!" I sat up. "This isn't like I got my period in gym class! This is *national television*. I've been totally humiliated—and it's just going to get worse!"

"Now you know how I feel," my mother whimpered, pulling a pillow over her head.

"Am I the only person who understands how horrible this is?" I shrieked. "Why are you two so dumb about this?"

"It's not that I'm dumb," my grandma said. "It's just that you don't have a choice." She sighed. "Look, your mother and I will look into some kind of alternative. But in the meantime you have to stick this out. You must go to school today, and every day, until we can figure something else out"

"You'd do that?" I asked.

"I'm not promising anything," she warned.

"But how do I get through today?"

Grandma shrugged. "Your mother got through natural childbirth. You'll find a way."

So there you have it: Sometimes Grandma can be somewhat understanding, if not cool. The result was the same, though. I was going to have to face the music. I have no idea what that expression means or where it came from, but whatever music the songwriter was facing, it must've been really terrible. Maybe it was a KISS concert.

Grandma dropped me at school on her way to work at the bank. I looked up at the wide, sprawling, tan-brick building like it was the mouth of hell. Then I took a deep breath and went inside.

The camera crew was on me like cat hair. I was their newest prime-time star, after all. And they wanted to catch every moment of my day.

Which was about to start. For real. Claire was across the main atrium, glaring at me, just waiting for me to show up so she could create her big scene. And ohhh, was she ready for her close-up.

"Oh, look, the big fat *whore* has arrived," she shouted, her voice projecting and echoing through the cavernous room.

I stopped in my tracks. "I didn't know you were dating him," I said.

"Oh, no?" Claire strolled toward me. I could see she had dressed up for this. She wore a studiously casual ensemble of fitted faux-army pants, an undersize "Free Winona" T-shirt, and Skechers sneakers. All put together with the meticulous care of a punk-rock teenage Edith Head. Her makeup was extra heavy, and every word out of her mouth sounded canned, like she'd written it down and rehearsed it in front of the mirror a thousand and one times.

"I don't know what kind of woman stoops so low that she has to steal another woman's man," she said.

"Ugh." I rolled my eyes. "Paging Dr. Phil. You can't *steal* a human being, Claire. Joey has a mind of his own."

"Oh, he *does*, does he?"

"Yeah, he does. What he doesn't have is a conscience, apparently. He played us both."

"Oh, he *did,* did he?"

"Yes!" Ugh! I guess this was Claire's way of getting a little extra time to think of what she'd say next. She asked a question, then left a dramatic pause. Right now I could practically see the wheels turning furiously inside her head. Finally her eyes snapped back up to meet mine and I could see she'd finally thought of a comeback. "Well . . . he may have a mind of his own, but he's not going to be thinking about *you* anymore."

"Fine." I shrugged.

"Don't act like this is no big deal!" she suddenly shrieked. She pointed a finger at my face and got in really close. "You messed up! You messed up big-time! And I'm going to get you back for this. You're going to be sorry you ever crossed me!" Her last words were a roar. All I could see was her giant face, almost slamming into mine as she screamed. It was so completely weird and shocking, I almost laughed.

Just as quickly, she was gone, stalking away from me toward, I guess, her first class. The cameras kept staring in my direction. I didn't know what to do, so I just looked down toward my feet until they got bored and went away. Slowly the rest of the kids in the atrium wandered off, along with the cameramen who'd captured every moment. I swallowed hard, my face burning.

Joey. I was going to kill him.

No, wait. Joey was just the pawn. It was Mike Millman I really wanted to kill. And I was going to find him.

"That went as well as it could," Pete said, coming up to me. My eyes were starting to burn from the tears I was holding back, and my chin was giving a distressing little wobble.

"I looked like an idiot," I said in a quavery voice.

"Nah. If you'd taken the bait, you'd have looked like an idiot. You really just looked like a girl having a bad day."

I looked up at him. "You think?"

He gave me a decisive nod. "I know." He looked back over his shoulder at the hallway where Claire had disappeared, then up at the camera over our heads. He took my arm and led me away from it a little.

"Look," he said. "Claire's a great person—we go way back, from being in school productions together. Theater geeks, you know."

"You're friends with that psycho?"

"She's not a psycho. But she is a little dramatic." I looked at him. "Okay. A lot dramatic. She's just always been that way. She doesn't mean anything by it. In fact, I feel like you guys would get along if you weren't being immortalized on video every five seconds."

"Huh," I said. "I don't know."

"I'm sure this'll blow over. Just try not to hold it against her, okay?"

I thought about it. The reality show had a way of turning up the volume on life in general. And Pete was a sensible guy, on the whole. I didn't feel particularly charitable toward Claire, but for the sake of my friendship with Pete I agreed.

"Fine. I'll try to keep an open mind when it comes to Claire Marangello," I said.

"Atta girl," he cheered. "Now come on; I'll walk you to French."

"Ohmigod, please don't say 'French,'" I begged. "French-kissing is what got me into this."

"Funny," Pete said. "You ever think of going on TV?"

Ha.

"I need to speak to Mike Millman."

"He's busy," the production assistant, all clunky glasses and bad attitude, told me.

The producers of the show had taken over a block of classrooms at the back of school. The only way to get in was through a huge set of metal doors that looked like they'd be more useful at Sing-Sing than in a public high school.

They bolted straight across, and you had to turn a little wheel to unbolt them; then they *creeeeaked* open with a groan that made you think you were about to come face-to-face with Count Chocula. I don't know why they were installed in the first place—maybe the door manufacturer was the mayor's brother-in-law. But it was helping the production crew maintain a level of security—and mystique—that Madonna would kill for.

As it opened, though, no bats flew out, and no monsters emerged. Well, no obvious monsters. Just this crabby PA. You know, Crankenstein. Inside, past her head, I could see a kabillion monitors and much rushing-about activity. Plus enough wires to run cable to the Australian outback.

"I don't care if he's on the phone to Howard Stern. I want him out here."

"You're going to have to—"

"It's all right." Mike stepped into view, and the production assistant flounced off in a huff. (For the record, you shouldn't flounce anywhere, especially in a huff, unless you're actually wearing crinolines. In black jeans, it just looks stupid.)

"What can I do for you?" he asked, with that

knowing, snaky smirk of his. Ugh, I just wanted to smack him so hard!

"Like you don't know," I snapped.

"What?" He shrugged. "I thought it was good."

"Take me off your stupid show," I said, seething. "I can't believe what you did to me. You've totally ruined my life. Just stop filming me."

"Ohhh, I can't do that," he said. "I can't do that at all. The public has spoken, and they want as much of you as they can get."

"Well, I *don't want them to have me*!" I said through clenched teeth.

"Nothing I can do," he said. "It's out of my hands."

I was so steamed. "This is a total humiliation," I spat. "Everyone's seeing me get screamed at. I didn't even come on to Joey. He came on to me. You made it look like I was throwing myself at him."

"You're playing this all wrong." Mike moved closer to me. Intimately closer. I tried to stay focused on my extreme anger. But he was *awfully* close. "The ratings are huge. I mean, through the roof. And that means people are watching—a lot of people. And *that* means a whole lot of attention is focused on you."

"Yessss," I hissed. "I am aware of that. But guess what, Mike? I'm an only child. I don't crave attention. I want to be left alone to blunder through the most awkward years of my life in peace."

"Don't you see what's going on? You're getting the kind of publicity for free that most people have to pay a bundle for," he whispered. "Who cares what they're saying as long as they're talking? It's all in how you use it. Parlay it right, and this exposure could get you everything you want."

"I just told you what I want," I told him.

"Oh, please," he said. "Only child, my ass. You want what every girl your age wants: fame, money, and a shot at the big time."

"I'd rather just get off your radar."

He sighed. "I can see you're angry."

"That's very astute."

"I'll tell you what. How about I make it up to you? I'll drive you home after school, so you don't have to ride the bus."

"I wouldn't get in your car—"

"Fine, how about a trip back to the city?"

That stopped me in my tracks. Back to the city. Even if it was only for a night, what heaven that would be. I could soak up the diesel fumes from the buses, take a walk through Washington Square Park, feel the reassuring pressure of concrete beneath my feet. He was right. There was no way out of this year of high school, and the fame that accompanied it. But I could lose myself in the anonymity of urban life for just a moment.

"When?" I asked, not even looking him in the eye.

"Saturday. We'll do it Saturday."

"It's not enough. I want you to stop making me look like an asshole."

"I'll have to see what I can do. It's kind of out of my hands." He shrugged. "I can't promise you anything. Except that I'll try."

It was all the satisfaction I was going to get. I closed my eyes and nodded.

"Fine," I said.

It would have to do for now.

Of course, I was going to have to face Joey sometime. And English class was the most obvious place to do that. The trouble was, everyone was hyperaware of us. Their eyes might be focused up front, at the teacher, but their ears were trained like little radar receivers right in our direction.

As if that weren't bad enough, Mrs. Lewinson—who seemed to have taken an instant dislike to me, I guess on account of my flirting with Joey on the first day of class—decided to torture me by insisting I go back to my original seat, right next to him. She wouldn't hear of my moving.

"You seemed to enjoy it last week," she said with studied innocence.

Bleah!

Joey didn't object at all. He just sat there next to me, not even pretending to pay attention to class. He just turned his big looming oval head toward me. I could see him perfectly out of my peripheral vision, floating there like a big unfestive balloon. I imagined myself with a giant hatpin, popping his stupid head. That almost made me forget how miserable I was.

"I'm sorry," he whispered.

Uccch. So much for feeling better.

"I don't want to hear it."

"But I'm really sorry. I acted like an asshole."

"Still are."

"I'm not. I'm trying to talk to you about it."

"Not talking." I raised my hand. Mrs. Lewinson called on me.

"She dies in childbirth," I said, in answer to

the question she'd just asked about the book we were reading. "Catherine dies in childbirth in an Italian hospital. Which never would have happened if she'd stayed the hell away from Frederick Henry in the first place," I continued, glaring daggers at Joey.

"Thank you, Miss O'Hara, but I meant for you to tell us what happens to Catherine in this chapter. You've just ruined the ending of the book for everyone."

I looked back at her. The same daggers I had been directing at Joey were now being pointed at me. Ouch.

"Sorry," I said.

"Thanks a *lot*," a girl in the second row muttered, blinking her mascara-laden eyelashes in my general direction.

"Oh, shut up," I snapped. "How long does it take you people to read a book, anyway? Did it ever occur to you to read this thing at home and discuss it in class instead of having your hands held through every chapter?"

"That's enough," Mrs. Lewinson barked at me. Second-row Girl shot me her version of a withering glare, which looked more like a bad case of gas. I gave a deep sigh and stared at the floor. Why is everything going wrong for me?

Was I a bad person in my last life? I wondered. Was I Hitler? Stalin? The guy who invented SPAM? What did I do to deserve this?

Nothing was going right. But that wasn't my only problem. I was starting to notice a distressing source of heat to my right. Joey's big, hateful balloonhead was still evoking a response in me. To my intense shame and horror, I realized that a part of me—oh, what the hell, the whole me—was *glad* he was looking at me. Pleased that he was sitting so close. Intensely aware of his presence as if I still had the hots for him.

Oh! God*damn* it! I did still have the hots for him!

Human chemistry is screwy! I'm serious. Here was a guy who I knew was a player, lied like a rug, didn't care about anyone but his stupid self. Yet my body yearned for him, and my brain wasn't helping the situation by replaying our kiss over and over and over again on the projection screen inside my skull.

I tried to shrink down into my seat. Now I really hated him. Because I wanted him more than anything.

"Fiona," he whispered. "Please. Let me make it up to you."

"Shut up."

"I want to break up with Claire. I've been trying to do it for months."

"Yeah, I saw you struggling with that. Every time you tried to talk to her, your tongue fell down her throat."

He gave an exasperated sigh. "I was . . . That was nothing but habit," he said. "She's a pretty girl, I'm not going to deny that. But she's nuts."

"No kidding," I told him. "Then again, dating a guy who lies to your face can make you a little crazy."

"Are you kidding? How do you break up with someone so emotional? I just haven't wanted to face her wrath. She's too much. I want to be with someone less emotional. Someone with a real head on their shoulders. Someone like you."

"Wow, you really make me sound attractive," I complained, giving him my own withering glare/bad-gas face. "Good old reliable Fiona. Almost as attractive as Kate Jackson, the plain Charlie's Angel. Can we drop this?"

"No!" Now that Joey had my attention, he wasn't letting it go. "I'm breaking up with her. Then I'll be all yours. If you'll let me, I'll make it up to you by being the best boyfriend the world has ever seen."

"Mr. Maynard," Mrs. Lewinson called out.

"What?"

"If it's not too much trouble."

"*What*?"

"It's your turn to read."

Joey scrambled for his copy of the book, peering over at the next desk to find the right page. I took the opportunity to try to screw my head back on straight. Why was I even listening to this bull? Once a player, always a player. A leopard can't change its spots. Cheated on her, he'll cheat on you. Every cliché dating back to the dawn of bad boyfriends kept flicking through my head like self-help flash cards.

Not to mention, how could I possibly date him when Claire would surely stalk me to death before we could go to our first movie?

It was crazy. As Joey's droning speed-reading drew to a close, I opened my copy of Hemingway and read my two-page requirement in a mumbled monotone. And thank the Lord, the bell finally rang.

"Fiona. Fiona!" Joey tried to get me to slow down as I shot out of the room. I made sure to slip out the door just before a clot of people, so he couldn't follow me. It was amazing. Once I was out of his presence, Joey's spell was broken. If I could just stay the hell away from him, and the temptation that surrounded him like a halo of Drakkar Noir, I'd be fine.

Not great, but fine.

Okay, not fine, either. But at least I wouldn't get involved with a total and complete snake, with a psycho ex-girlfriend that's not yet his ex-girlfriend, on national TV. And that, for now, would have to be enough.

You know life's bad when you start looking forward to calculus as a nice distraction. Let's face it: It's a class full of math geeks that's so difficult, I have to spend the entire period concentrating just to keep from falling behind. It was one of the few classes this school seemed to keep at a respectable academic level. Or maybe I just suck at math. Either way, I was grateful for every number, letter, and squiggle as I sank into my chair.

That is, until I noticed a new student in the class.

Baxter. Was that his name? Yeah, Baxter. That big, stupid, beefy football player who'd been menacing Pete the day I met him. He galumphed into class five minutes late, his sheer bulk taking up more room in the classroom than all the rest of us put together. He looked like a different species of human from the wispy, bespectacled people that surrounded him.

I noticed he was walking with a limp, gingerly favoring his right leg. It looked really painful.

Good, I thought. I hope it hurts like hell. Guess he decided to pick on someone his own size for a change.

Then I had to wonder where he found anyone his own size. The gorilla cage at the zoo?

He gimped up to Mr. Merino's desk. The teacher was as wispy and tiny as anyone else in the class. The only difference, really, was that he'd managed to grow a mustache and had lost a bit of hair. He was clearly a little hostile to the cornerback (or whatever) invading his classroom, and did his best to embarrass Baxter.

"Can I help you?" he asked, like he was sure the kid was lost.

"I'm transferring into this class," Baxter mumbled, dropping a slip of pink paper on the desk. Mr. Merino blinked uncomprehendingly.

"*This* class?" he asked.

"Calculus?"

"Yes."

"Then, yeah. This class." Baxter stood there, not sure what to do next.

"Well, suit yourself," Mr. Merino said, waving toward an empty seat. There were plenty. "I'm sure this'll be straightened out soon."

Jeez! The poor guy, I caught myself thinking. Then I remembered: I hated the big oaf too. So I went back to taking notes, and tried not to wonder what the heck he was doing there. It was weird.

I couldn't help but sneak a peek at the guy about halfway through class. He had his notebook open and a pencil poised, but his face—especially his eyes—was etched with terror. He was totally and completely at sea. But that's all I had time to notice. I had to turn my attention back to Mr. Merino and focus on every word that came out of his mouth or I'd be joining Baxter in the leaky lifeboat of noncomprehension.

At the end of class I stood and started walking out the door, shaking my head to loosen the numbers lodged in various corners. So I didn't notice the humongous barrel chest blocking out the sun until I almost bumped into it.

"You're Fiona," Baxter said.

"Ah . . . yeah," I answered.

"So. Hi."

"Hi. Excuse me." I tried to walk around him.

"Can I . . . uh . . . "

"What?" I asked sharply. "What's up? You going to kick *my* ass now? You're done picking on kids with glasses and you want to move on to beating up girls?"

"I, uh . . . " Baxter didn't have a comeback for that one. He didn't have a comeback for anything. This was too easy.

"Can I go, please?" I asked. "I've got somewhere to be."

"Yeah."

He stepped aside and I sprinted out of the room. Creepy! What the hell did that no-brain hunk of muscle want with me? Was this whole school populated with nincompoops?

And if so, could someone please get me out of here?

"So that was my first day back," I said to Pete as we strolled away from the school. I had to admit, the winding streets past proto-Victorian houses were kind of pretty. In the same way that a mushroom cloud is pretty, I guess. "Total and utter hell every way I turned."

"Well, you survived," Pete said with a shrug.

"Yes, I survived. There's that." I gave a decisive nod. "Now I never have to do it again, right?"

"Not till tomorrow."

"Ohhhh!" I smacked myself in the forehead. "Tomorrow! I forgot about that. It's Friday, right?"

"Tuesday."

"Aaagh!" I put my hands around Pete's neck and gave him a mini-strangle. "What kind of friend are you if you won't rip the space-time continuum for me?"

"Man, you're like some kind of geek-in-hiding." Pete giggled, pushing me off. "That's what they should call the show. *The Secret Geek*. 'She wears Prada—but she loves Chewbacca. Which side will prevail?'"

"Oh, go play in traffic." I laughed.

"Wuh-oh," Pete bleated.

"What?"

"Looks like Han Solo just showed up in the *Millennium Falcon*."

I looked up and saw Millman pulling up in that little convertible of his. "Oh, what does he want?" I wondered as I stepped over to him.

"You want that ride?" he asked me.

"I'm walking with my friend," I said.

"He won't mind. Right, Pete?"

Pete just shrugged. "It's up to her," he said.

"I'd rather walk. On coals, barefoot."

"Come on." He leaned over and pushed open the passenger door. "I want to talk to you about the show."

"I've got nothing to say about that," I told him.

"I want to give you some insight."

"I got plenty of insight Friday night."

"Your friend can have a ride, too."

"Where, in the trunk?"

"Oh, go ahead," Pete told me. "I'll take the shortcut home, and you can tell me what he had to say."

I rolled my eyes. "Way to throw me to the lions," I complained.

"I want to see what happens!" He shoved me into the car and I closed the door behind me.

"Start driving. And talk fast," I said.

"I'm sorry," he said, as we pulled out.

"That's the second time today I've heard that," I said.

"I know, I saw the footage from your English class."

I gave an exasperated sigh. "Right. The footage. What are you trying to do to me?"

"I'm trying to— Jeez!" Millman shook his head. "Fiona, it's not that bad. You're playing this all wrong. You've got an amazing opportunity here. Do you understand that? You've got your allotted fifteen minutes of fame. Don't you want to parlay it into something greater?"

"Like what, a shot at *Hollywood Squares*?"

"I'm serious! Fiona, you have something. A spark, a sparkle. That's what we saw when we made you the main character. And other people are going to see it, too. Now you can take this and run with it, or you can drop the ball."

I looked down at my lap. "Despite your hackneyed metaphors, I do understand what you're saying," I said. "But this isn't what I want. I just want to go back to the city and live my little anonymous life. I don't belong in this town, and I don't belong on TV."

"But TV is where you are," Millman said, pulling over in front of my house. He turned to look at me. "Life's going to throw you curveballs, little girl. You can dodge them, or you can catch them and throw them back. If you want, you can really take this thing all the way."

I had to admit, he sounded sincere. He just had totally weird and skewed values.

"I'll think about it," I said.

"You promise?"

"I promise."

"We still on for that trip back to the city?"

"I thought you were kidding!"

"Nope. I do feel bad. My wheels are at your disposal. You've got a whole day of seeing old friends, riding the subway, and swilling latte at Café Borgia, if that's what floats your boat."

"I'd really love that," I admitted as I got out of the car. "Really."

"Okay, then." Mike drove off, and Pete tumbled out of a hedge next to my house.

"Well?" he asked.

"He's convinced I'm going to be the next Jennifer Love Hewitt."

"Yikes, one is enough," Pete huffed, waving a hand in front of his face. "Come on; I'm going to make popcorn. If your life's going to turn into a movie, I want to be prepared in my front-row seat."

I followed him inside, but not before looking back over my shoulder at Millman's retreating sports car. Well, he's interesting, I thought. I'm not sure what he's up to, but it's definitely interesting.

That night the three of us were enjoying a lovely repast of egg noodles and stew, courtesy of Mary Dolan. She'd stopped by yet again, poking around, trying to interest my mother in some lame social activity like bowling or garage-sale-ing, but of course my mom had given her the big freeze again. I felt bad for her, but I couldn't blame Mom, either. The woman had all the charm of a chipmunk. And the tenacity of a terrier. And the cooking skills of a . . . Oh, you get the idea.

The phone rang. Mom stood up and answered it, then dropped the receiver on the floor and stomped down into the basement, slamming the door behind her.

"I thought I was the teenager," I said to Grandma.

"And I thought I was going to retire this year," she said.

I leaned down and picked up the phone. "Dad?"

"Yeah, it's me," he said.

I twisted my fork around in my noodles. "Nice of you to keep in touch."

"I haven't exactly been welcome around there."

"Mom's not the only one in this house."

"I'm sorry."

I sighed. "How are you doing? You sound tired."

"I'm pretty exhausted. But I think I found an

apartment. It's here in Queens, but at least it'll be mine. Then you can come visit. I'm sorry about the other weekend."

"That'd be great." Yeah. Queens. An outer borough. Like Brooklyn, but without the charm. Still, it was on the right side of the Hudson.

"At least it's not Staten Island," he said, reading my mind. I had to laugh.

"Mom's gone off the deep end," I said.

"She's always been crazy."

"Yeah, Dad, like you helped that situation a lot," I pointed out. "And now she's dragging me with her. I'm in hell out here. Didn't you see the show?"

"I saw it," he said. "It looked like it was really stressful for you. I would have called earlier, but I wasn't sure how to handle it myself."

I turned farther away from Grandma and leaned forward, over the sink. "Can you hear me?" I said in a low voice.

"Yes," he said, dubiously.

"I was thinking you could . . . you could use this," I said, feeling like the low-down dirty traitor I was.

"Use what?"

"Use the show. To get custody." Now I was whispering. "Of *me*. You can say it's not safe for me here. You can say I'm being exploited. I can come back to the city and I'll go back to Stuyvesant. The judge'll have to listen. All you do is show them a tape of the show, I'll back you up. . . ."

The silence on the other end of the line was deafening.

"Fee," he finally said, using the diminutive only my parents were allowed to call me. Everything in his voice screamed, "I'm about to turn you down."

"Don't," I interrupted quickly. "Forget it. Don't say another word. I don't want to hear you say no."

"I just can't do that." He sighed. "I can't go any deeper in debt to my lawyer. The last round of negotiations cleaned me out, and all I got out of it was that I had to buy your mom that Passat. I already went through the whole custody thing. I can't afford to fight anymore."

"Nobody told you to fight like that in the first place," I pointed out. "You hired the first lawyer; you sued Mom for the armoire. You could have bought three for the money you spent on that one."

"I'm not saying I'm perfect. I made mistakes too. And the upshot is I can't afford another day in court."

"Fine."

"And this place is just a studio. Not even a one-bedroom. You wouldn't even have your own bed, let alone your own room."

"Sure, yeah."

"Fee, don't be angry—"

"Why would I be angry? You can fight with mom for months over knickknacks, but when it comes to helping your own daughter, you suddenly put the brakes on?"

"It's not that I don't want you here—"

"It's just that I don't fit into your midlife crisis. God, this is so Lifetime Television for Women. Dad, don't be such a stereotype."

"Fee." He sighed. "It's not like that."

"No? What's it like then?"

"Come on. It's only for a year. By the time you're a senior, I'm sure things will have worked themselves out."

"How?" I asked. "You're both in debt up to your armpits. The only hope I have of going to college is if I get a scholarship, and with the academics at this school, and the distraction of this show, that's becoming more and more unlikely. Your decision to be too exhausted to fight comes at the exact same time that I need you to put up your dukes, Dad. For *me*."

"I'm sorry."

"I don't care." I groaned, too tired to shout. I was too tired to even really get mad. I really, honestly didn't care. I stood up and stared out the window into the backyard, acutely aware that my grandma was watching my every move.

"I don't care," I repeated weakly. "This is too much. Everything's too much, Dad."

"I'm sorry. I'm really sorry," he said. "If only you hadn't signed a release. If you'd have asked me, I would've told you not to."

"Yeah, well, I would have asked you if you—Wait a minute. What did you just say about a release?"

"Yeah. It's a form you sign giving them permission to use you on TV. They probably had you sign it on the first day of school without even explaining it."

"Wait. I remember. Millman said something about the releases—but I never had a chance to sign mine."

"You didn't?"

"No. No, I didn't. Is that bad?"

My dad laughed. "It's bad for this Millman guy, whoever he is."

"Why? What do you mean?"

Dad let out a whooping yell. "Fiona, it means they broadcast you illegally. It means you can shut them down and probably own the network if you want."

"Are you serious?"

"Well, I'm overstating a little, but it's a very big deal. They really screwed up. You can get them to do just about anything you want at this point."

"Ohhh!" I put my hand over my mouth. I didn't even know where to look.

"What's wrong?" Grandma said. "What did he say to you? Are you all right?"

I hugged her so hard, I probably broke a rib. "Oh, Grandma, it's great!"

"Oh!" she squeaked. "Oh, well, that's good then!"

"It's good!" I laughed. "It's good. Dad, that's really good."

"Do you want me to talk to my lawyer?"

"No! No, we can't afford that," I said. "I don't want to sue. I don't want to shut down production. I've got a better idea. Oh! Oh, Dad, this is cool."

"Then I'm back in your good graces?"

I thought of my mom, lying downstairs in her never-ending funk. I thought of my own snake-like behavior, trying to abandon her out here in

Jersey, and felt a wave of guilt. "I don't know if you're totally in yet," I told him. "But you do get to stay my dad for one more week."

"Oh. Phew," he said.

"I have to tell Pete."

"That's not the guy in the library?"

"*No*! That guy's a creep."

"Should I call Uncle Malachy to kick his ass?"

"Not yet, but maybe soon," I told him.

"Just let me know."

"Okay. I've got to go, Dad."

"All right. I e-mailed you my new number. Call me whenever you want."

"Okay. Okay. Dad?"

"Yeah?"

"Thanks a lot."

"Well . . . it was the least I could do."

"Yeah, kinda. But thanks anyway."

The next morning, Pete and I marched up to the Doors of Doom, our shoulders squared off, ready for battle.

Mike responded to our knock himself.

"Hey," he said. "You look mad."

"I'm not mad," I told him. "I'm here to talk business."

I walked in the door like I owned the place. Because you know what? I pretty much did.

The Real Deal: Episode Two
Review in the **Daily Post**

Hamilton High: The Wildest Ride in Reality T.V.

For those of you accustomed to turning to this page and seeing a review of a different show each week, I apologize. I could have written a review of the updated version of My Favorite Martian *that debuted last night. In fact, I did. Then I saw last night's episode of* The Real Deal *and scrapped the whole thing. In fact, I actually stopped the presses.*

I have a new obsession, and its name is Hamilton High.

For those of you who have been living under a rock, Hamilton High is the site of the newest reality series. Set in a New Jersey high school, it chronicles the misadventures of a misplaced misanthrope, known only as Fiona, who's utterly lost in an unbrave new world.

Well, this week, she got hers.

I don't know what on earth happened in the last week. I will say that the episode looks like it was reedited at the last possible second by a band of monkeys on crack. And boy, has Claire had the tables turned on her.

From the moment Fiona walks into the school, Claire behaves like a raving lunatic. At one point, when she's shouting at Fiona, Claire's eyes actually bug out of her head. I'm serious: right out of her head. She has no less than three different brokenhearted hissy fits. In one, she stops in the middle and begins again, as if she were playing a scene in a movie.

Meanwhile, a shocking secret is revealed. Her darling boyfriend, Joey—the devoted guy who we thought was being seduced by Fiona—turns out to be a massive player. Remember that lingering look at Fiona, as she awaits her ride at the end of last week? It never happens. And why? Because Joey is off romancing a naïve young member of the freshman class.

It's fascinating. It's horrendous. It's . . . it's brilliant TV. And it's going to be rebroadcast this Sunday night. So if you didn't TiVo it, you didn't tape it, you haven't seen it, make a date with your living room couch for that night. Because as Joey pathetically sniffs around Fiona, Claire slowly shows herself to be such a diva, the scorned-girlfriend thing loses all its steam.

The Real Deal Fan Forum

New Topic   Post Reply

Author: JoeyLuvr

Subject: I take it back!

Message: Daaaamn! Remember last week when I posted that Fiona is a skanky ho? I was wrong! Looks like Claire is a psycho hosebag of immense proportions. Sorry, Fiona, if you are reading this!!

Author: CouchTater

Subject: What is up with that girl?

Message: Somebody'd better tell Claire to check herself or else I'm-a be on the next bus to New Jersey! Fiona better b****-slap that ho or I'll do it for her!

Author: ChannelSurfer

Subject: Cut it out

Message: I think she needs help. You guys should stop calling her bad names. She needs compassion and understanding, because obviously she is emotionally retarded.

Author: CouchTater

Subject: Pleez

Message: I bet you wouldn't be so compassionate if it was your face she was all up in.

Author: MissMaisy
Subject: LOL
Message: Good one, Channel! As for me I can't wait to see how Fiona handles this one. If I were her I think I'd have given up by now. I feel bad for her. I thought she was a ho at first too, but now Joey's obviously such a playa, and I believe she didn't know.

Author: JoeyLuvr
Subject: Who cares!!
Message: All I know is Claire's a b**** and she should be embarrassed! She should get homeschooled for the rest of her life! ROTFLMAO!!!!

chapter FOUR

I'm bad, right?

I don't care.

I didn't want to shut down production. I knew the school actually needed the money, and anyway, I'm pretty sure I couldn't really do that. And even if I didn't care about being on the show, it was clear that the other kids did. I mean, Pete tried out for *American Idol*, for God's sake. I was stuck at this school, and if word got out I was the one responsible for taking everyone off the air, they'd really hate my guts.

Did I feel bad about selling out Claire? The truth is, yeah. She and Pete were old friends, and now their friendship was kind of on the rocks because of me. And I could understand why she hated me—I'd hate me too, if I were her. On the other hand, if she hadn't given me the livid freakout in front of the cameras in the first place, she wouldn't have been such an obvious choice for New Villain. So a part of me felt like she was getting a little spoonful of her own medicine.

And man, it must have tasted bitter. Because the look on her face Monday morning was extremely sour.

She scuttled into school at the last possible second, going straight to French class with no chitchat, no hanging out, not even a trip to her locker. She sat in the back with her head down, apparently completely baffled as to how to deal with her new notoriety. I didn't want to make things worse by trying to have some kind of conversation as three cameras looked on, so I just left her there, hoping the producers would leave her alone. I'd try to talk to her later—or let Pete try to smooth things over a little.

Meanwhile, people were ten thousand times more friendly to me.

"Hi," Judy Kreiger said to me, with a crinkly-nosed smile. "I think we got off on the wrong foot. I'm sorry I made fun of your clothes."

"Oh. Well, I apologize for that Wal-Mart crack," I told her. "I don't usually get catty like that."

"Oh, it was totally deserved," she said, waving her hand as if to clear the air of any remaining bad feelings. "Anyway, if you want to sit with us at lunch, you're totally welcome to."

"That's nice," I said. "I usually hang out with Pete, though."

"Bring him too!"

Mrs. Cohen started class, and I shook my head. What was it? Did my role as innocent victim suddenly give me a magnetic personality?

Or was Judy just hoping for some screen time? Totally weird.

It was like that all day, though. People approached me and chatted, their eyes flickering off to the sides in a self-conscious way. Two cameras loomed around me at all times. Boy, you'll never walk alone if you're on reality TV, I'll tell ya.

Not that that made me feel any friendlier toward the burgh I inhabited. These people were . . . ugh. All the men did was play golf, watch golf, and drink bad coffee out of golf-themed mugs. And the women seemed to go straight from eighteen to fifty when they got married. Something spooky happened to them right after their weddings: They all got the same haircut, gained twenty pounds, and forgot they'd ever had an ounce of individualism. Sexiness went right out the window. They all looked like Mary Dolan, and Mary Dolan embodied everything wrong with Hamilton, New Jersey. Everything my mom had run away from, and everything I refused to become. Which was why I had to get the eff out of there, ay-sap. Which was why I went looking for Mike as soon as I could.

I knocked on the big metal doors that separated the City of Production from the rest of the school. That same pissed-looking production assistant opened it. I don't know if she was suffering perma-PMS or what. It was like the lenses of her chunky glasses were little rectangles of hostility. Even the stripes on her tights seemed irritated.

"Yah," she said.

"I need to talk to Millman," I said.

"Are you sure that's a good idea?" she asked, giving me the once-over. I'd been once-overed by bigger snobs than her, though. I stood my ground.

"It seems to have worked out okay for me so far," I informed her, and watched a look flicker across her face that I couldn't quite place.

"Just watch out for yourself, okay?" she said, softening momentarily to the consistency of a pinewood bat instead of a concrete block.

I nodded. "Don't worry. I can handle him."

"Uh-huh. Yeah," she said. Then she shrugged and turned around for a second, yelling behind her.

Then Mike was there.

Something was just like . . . different about him. I think it was the way he was looking at me. Like he hadn't really seen me before, and now that he knew who I was, he was totally fascinated. Well, that sounds kind of conceited—maybe I was just reading into it. But there was definitely a different vibe going on. His face sort of lit up.

Maybe mine did too.

He stepped out of the production area and closed the door behind him. He and I were pretty much alone in the hallway.

"So what did you think?" he asked.

"I didn't say you had to humiliate her," I couldn't help blurting out.

"No, but it was a nice touch, right?"

I shrugged. "I'd be lying if I didn't admit that it felt good, but it was a little over the top. Didn't they teach you subtlety at whatever film school you went to?"

He leaned into me. "I couldn't help it," he said. "The story just blossomed once I put you in the middle of it. I should thank you. I didn't see it before, but now I know exactly how the whole season's going to go."

"Whatever. We had a deal."

He shrugged. "That was for Saturday."

"I want to go now. Today. After school."

"Are you kidding? I have a job to do."

"Yeah? You won't have much of one if the new star of your show doesn't sign her release."

Agh! I couldn't believe I'd said such a thing. I

sounded like such a diva! But if Mike thought I was tacky, he didn't show it. He just gave me a slow, sexy head shake, never taking his blue eyes off me. "You are one amazing girl," he said. "We'll have to start out right after the last class to make it in before rush hour."

"I know where your car's parked," I told him. "I'll see you there at two-thirty-two."

The rest of the day passed in sort of a blur. I noticed a few things—like the way you start to forget cameras are filming you, after they've been trailing you for a week or so. Especially if you're no longer worried they're going to make a fool of you.

Maybe I was getting bigheaded. Full of myself. I don't know. It does something to you, being on TV. Even if you grew up around it and you think it won't. It wasn't like I was like, "Oh, I'm a big TV star." It was just all that ass kissing. People acting nice to me all of a sudden, for the first time that year. I guess I hadn't noticed how lonely I'd been feeling until people actually started being friendly toward me.

Anyway, it made me feel like I could do anything. Like get in a car with a guy I didn't really know, who was old enough to be . . . too old.

I mean, yeah, he was hot. But there's a reason those laws are in place, you know. I'd told that production assistant I could handle him, and I felt like I could. But that look on her face should have told me there was more to him than I realized.

Anyway, I met Millman at his sporty little car—this time I noticed it was a Nissan, for those of you who are interested, and it had these cool sideways doorhandles—and we drove through town in five seconds flat. I was so excited. I fiddled with the radio, turned the air conditioner on and off a few times, inspected myself in the little mirror hidden on the other side of the visor over my head. I wanted to make sure I didn't have Magic Helmet Head or Sudden Stirrup Pants Disease. I was afraid Jersey would cling to me like the stench of perfume strips clings to fashion magazines. I seemed to look okay. Then again, I might be looking at myself with Jersey eyes, I thought. That cracked me up.

"What's so funny?" Millman shot me an amused glance.

"God, nothing, I just can't wait."

"What do you want to do when we get there?"

"Just soak it up. I don't even want to call anyone. I'll stop by the Starbucks where everyone goes after school, surprise them. I want to feel that reassuring, solid-feeling concrete under my feet. Pretend everything's okay for an afternoon."

"This has been tough on you. The move."

I looked out my window. "I mean, it wasn't my first choice. It wasn't my choice at all." Then I shrugged off the heavy feeling that settled around my heart. "I don't want to think about that," I told him. "I'm just going to enjoy my afternoon. After all, I've earned it."

He gave a little snicker. "I guess you did," he said. "You earned a couple things."

"What's that supposed to mean?"

He just gave an annoyingly mysterious shrug.

Yes, I hear them: alarm bells are ringing like crazy. Red flags are flying all around me. But I just wanted to get back to the city so badly. See my friends and feel something familiar. I didn't want to admit how gross this all was. Until it was almost too late.

We were on the turnpike and I could see the Empire State Building, standing like a tall man in a gray flannel suit among the different heights and styles of the buildings around it. So solid and real. I couldn't take my eyes off it—until I felt the car swerve off the road and into a parking lot.

"What are we doing here?" I asked. I looked up. "We're at a mall," I said. "This is the mall. Why are we stopping? Are you getting gas?"

But Millman steered his car to the outer reaches of the parking lot, where the yellow lines were nothing but an ironic reinforcement of the fact that there were no cars parked here. The mall loomed like a prefab mountain range behind us. We were facing trees. Woods. The Empire State Building was hidden by them.

I didn't like this.

Don't get me wrong: I'm not a prude. I like a good tongue-wrestle as much as the next girl, and one time I spent the night with Jason Saks, of the Saks Fifth Avenue family, in his parents' bed when they were out of town. We french-kissed the night away, and though we didn't do much more than that, I know what goes on between a guy and a girl when they both want to be there. But you know what? This was not where I wanted to be. Not with this guy. Something was definitely off about this whole situation.

Way off.

I turned to him, but he looked somehow different. The friendly, open face he'd shown me back at school was gone, replaced with a closed expression that looked distinctly demented.

"Come on now," he said, waggling an eyebrow at me. "You want that trip to the city, don't you?"

"Mike, cut it out," I said. "Come on, let's keep driving. You don't want to hit rush hour at the Lincoln Tunnel, do you?"

"That's up to you," he said. "We can do this fast, or we can . . . take our time."

Ugh! Where'd he hear that line? On some weird hybrid of *Blind Date* and *Cops*?

"Okay, Mike, I'm fully aware that this is going to upset you, and I'm sorry if I misled you in any way, but I am not going to make out with you."

"Make out!" He chuckled and shifted closer to me in the bucket seat. "That's so cute. Come on, Fiona. You know you're not like those other girls. You stand out in that school. It's like you're a natural leader. Let me take you all the way."

"All right! That's it!" I somehow spazzed out of my seatbelt and yanked the door handle.

Nothing happened.

I heard a chuckle. Ugh. I realized I was in one of those ultramodern cars where the driver controls the automatic locks, creating a hermetically sealed love nest. Or snake pit, depending on which seat you're sitting in. I was stuck.

But I had one more trick up my sleeve.

I whirled around to face Mike and stuck my index finger up to my mouth. It probably looked like I was pointing out a cold sore. He looked baffled.

"Look, mister," I said. "You are dealing with a girl who went to high school with the daughters of aging supermodels, social climbers, and depressed overachievers. Which means I can make myself barf in less time than it takes you to pay the check at Balthazar. Without even making my eyes water."

Mike bolted backward, plastering himself against the driver's-side door. Then he gave a nervous laugh. "You wouldn't do that," he said.

"Try me," I told him. I shoved my finger deeper into my mouth. It made it hard to talk, but my point was getting made. "We used to have speed-vomit contests during summer camp," I said, slurring the words around my outstretched finger.

"Hey, look, if I made a mistake, I'm sorry," he said, feeling behind him for the door-lock controls. "Just, ah . . . okay, look, just don't do that."

My finger tickled the back of my throat and I gave a long, lusty, disgusting gagging sound. It was like wet machinery. It even grossed me out, and I was doing it. Seeing visions of ruined tan upholstery, Mike finally found the control and popped the lock on my door. I opened it in a hurry and stepped out.

He zoomed backward out of the parking space and made a beeline for the exit, screeching his tires as he went. The passenger door was still open, flapping in the wind, and when he reached the distant exit back to the highway, I saw him reach across and slam it closed. The whole time I was grinning like an idiot.

Daughters of supermodels. What a jerk. Stuyvesant is a public school that you only get into if your brain has its own brain, not an Upper East Side private school. Despite my exposure to Becky's odd eating habits and troublingly frequent trips to the bathroom after a good meal, I couldn't have thrown up without the help of a stomach virus.

But hey, it worked. And as I watched him drive desperately away, I felt as triumphant as Ivana Trump contesting her prenup.

Then his car disappeared.

Then it wasn't so funny.

I felt a distinct deflation as I looked around me. The sun was still beaming cheerfully, and the wide parking lot looked like a model of suburban safety. But the mall was at least half a mile away. And once I got there, then what? Was I supposed to call my mom, who would replace my dad's ass platter with one I could call my very own? My grandma, who'd have a heart attack? My dad, who wouldn't answer his cell phone because he was either working, moving, or in his lawyer's office?

I couldn't worry about that. Leaving my momentary triumph behind me, I trudged up toward the mall, my chunky Steve Maddens clopping along on the asphalt. I kept my head bent down, so that when I glanced up, the mall would look a lot closer. After thirty *clop-clops*, I peeked up.

Jeez. It didn't appear any closer.

I looked behind me. The parking spot, skid marks marking the concrete, seemed impossibly far. Ugh, it was like the Trail of Sears. All I could do was keep moving toward the giant retail beacon of hope.

By the time I got to the main entrance of the mall, my feet were dotted with blisters, my calves ached, and my underarms were prickly with sweat. No wonder everyone in the suburbs was fat. You needed a car just to get from the parking lot to the department store. And, of course, now that I was here, I had no plan of action whatsoever. I was stuck in the middle of godforsaken New Jersey. Nobody knew where I was. I had nobody to call. I was all alone in the world.

"Fiona?"

I whirled around. Who was talking to me? Standing behind me was a big, beefy . . . Baxter?

"Oh, for God's sake!" I shrieked. I whirled around and stomped away from him. Where was I headed? Back out to the parking lot? I didn't know, but right at that moment he embodied everything—square, intolerant, and dumb—that I hated about my new life. I wasn't thinking clearly. I was having a tantrum, all right? It was all just too much, and he was the straw that broke this camel's emotional back.

"Fiona, wait—what's wrong?" I heard him say behind me. "What are you doing here?"

"Leave me alone," I said, trying to shove the door to the mall open. It wouldn't budge. I was too stressed out to notice I was shoving on a door that said *Pull*. And I heard a distressing wobble in my voice, as if I were going to . . . Oh no. I was going to cry.

"I've been meaning to talk to you," Baxter said, standing behind me. "Can't I just talk to you for a minute?"

I was so embarrassed I didn't want to turn around. I am not a crier by any means. But this was all too much. I hadn't had a chance to really feel everything that had happened to me—and as bad as everything was, today just trumped it all: the divorce, the move, the shitty school . . . Hell, even my old friends had deserted me in my time of need. The one thing I could rely on was myself. And I'd let myself down by stumbling into a dangerous and stupid situation. I felt my shoulders start to shake, and I bent my head down in a last-ditch effort to hide my ridiculously emotional reaction.

"Hey, are you . . . Hey, what's wrong?" Baxter put his big monkey paw on my shoulder. I twitched, trying to shake it off, but then he did something truly surprising. He put those big, beefy, muscle-arms around me, and pulled me in close, moving me away from the doors and just standing there quietly with me. And I was so tired, so forlorn, I let him do it—and you know what? He didn't feel like a gorilla. He felt more like a big bear. Despite myself, I relaxed for a moment, letting the sobs burble up out of me till there weren't any more, and I actually felt a lot better.

Of course, that left me with a face full of snot that was basically stuck to Baxter's T-shirt. I gave a long sigh, then started patting my pockets for a Kleenex or something. Baxter handed me a red bandanna, and I took it gratefully.

"Um, thanks," I said, giving a loud honk into the cotton fabric, then giving a halfhearted scrub to his besmirched T-shirt. "I'll wash this, okay?"

"It's fine; don't worry about it. What happened? Are you all right?"

"It's a long story," I told him. "I did a really stupid thing. I trusted somebody who didn't deserve it, and I'm . . . kind of stuck here."

"Well, no, you're not," Baxter said, giving me a little dah-hickey head waggle. "I'm here, and so's my truck, so that takes care of that."

"Oh. Oh! Oh, you're kidding!" I gasped. "I mean, obviously . . . I didn't even think!"

"Boy, for a smart girl—"

"Don't even. I'm having a bad day," I said.

Baxter looked out the window, studying the

skyline in the distance. "You were trying to get back to the city, weren't you?"

"Yeah."

"Let's go the rest of the way. You can show me around, tell me what happened."

"Are you serious? Don't you have something to do?"

"Yeah. I have to go into Manhattan." He ignored my dropped jaw and shrugged. "I came this far so I could go to this place." He swept his arm behind me, and I saw a store that mass-marketed tutoring services to the mall crowd. He stared at it sheepishly for a few moments, then turned back to me. "I thought they could help me, but they're really just for smaller kids, and the ones who are about to flunk out. Anyway, I figured as long as I was this close, I'd go visit someone I know there."

"But who—"

"Come on; let's get in the truck. I'll tell you on the way into Manhattan."

"I feel like I'm sitting in my living room, not in a car," I said, as we hummed up to the tunnel and Baxter paid the toll.

"It's a CR-V," he said, by way of explanation.

"Which means nothing to me," I told him.

"It's a little truck."

"It's nice." I bounced in my seat a little. "Huge, but nice."

"So what were you doing at that mall?" he asked.

I sighed. "It's so stupid. I'm such an idiot. That guy Millman, who works on the show? The assistant director or whatever? We've been sort of flirting. Except I didn't realize that's what was going on, if you can believe that. I was just trying to get myself out of hot water on the show. And I did that. But then he got the idea I was interested in him for more. He offered me a ride into the city, and I took it. And, well, before we got there he tried to . . . " My voice trailed off and I looked down.

Baxter was dumbfounded. "That jerk," he said. "You can have him arrested."

"Oh, he didn't really do anything," I said, waving him off. "Besides, I'd be humiliated if anyone knew how stupid I was. I just want the whole thing to go away."

He shook his head. "I don't know, Fiona. My sister told me that if guys get away with bad behavior, it just makes things worse for all the other women in the world."

"Who's your sister, Gloria Steinem?" I asked.

He shot me an uneasy look. "I don't know who that is," he said. "She goes to school in Manhattan, at this place uptown. Barnard College. She's the one I'm going to visit. She's a Women's Studies major. And she's got a lot of ideas. She says she's training me to be a decent human being. Keeps trying to get me off the football team. Well, I guess she got her wish on that one."

"Wait, what do you mean?"

He waved his hand at his left leg, which was stretched out under the dashboard as he used his right one to work the gas and brakes. "I blew out my knee," he said. "Stupid mistake. I went running in the snow all last winter, trying to stay in shape, and it got weaker and weaker. Then I played on a rugby team this summer, and bam. No more left knee. Coach is furious at me. So are my parents. Football was my ticket to college."

"Oh. That's a drag," I said.

He grimaced. "It's worse than a drag," he said. "I've been concentrating on football all these years—not on schoolwork. My dad's always had it in his head that I'd go to Princeton. There's no way I'll get in now. When I realized I couldn't play football anymore, I tried to transfer back into the smart classes. Dammit, I knew my sister was right when she said I had to pay attention to schoolwork too. Now it looks like it's too late. I can't keep up. At this rate, I'll be lucky if I get into Rutgers."

"I'm so sorry," I told him. I was. Poor big doofy dummy. Except I was starting to wonder if he was as big a doof as I'd thought.

"Do you have anywhere in particular you want to go?" he asked.

"I don't know. I was going to head down to my high school—I mean my old one," I said. "It's all the way downtown. But I don't think I can actually deal with that right now. I look terrible, and I don't know what I'd say to everyone. Besides—ugh. I'm sure they've seen the show, and the fact that they didn't even bother to call just makes me think they're embarrassed to know me, or they've forgotten I ever existed." I sat back, rolling down the window to take in the diesel-scented air and let the humid grime settle on my face. It was a warm autumn, the best kind. "I'm just happy to be here. Go wherever you want."

We headed up Broadway. As Baxter dialed his cell phone to let his sister know he was almost there, I was sitting there enjoying the ride, but also trying to fit a couple puzzle pieces together in my brain. Something wasn't adding up, and it was bothering me. Baxter seemed really decent. And if what he said was true, he at least had the potential to take the honors classes that would get him to a good school. His sister went to Barnard, a smart-girl school that was part of Columbia University. What was he doing trying to gay-bash Pete?

When we got to the heavy iron gates, decorated with a bronze dancing bear, in front of the white-columned main building, a girl in a flannel shirt, black plaid skirt, and Doc Martens came running around to Baxter's side of the car. Her long black ponytail whipped out behind her, and she brushed her thick bangs aside.

"Doofus!" she said, conking Baxter on the head. So I wasn't the only one who thought so! "Who's the dish?" she asked, peering across the car at me.

"Fiona, this is my sister, Deb. Deb, this is Fiona," he said, nodding toward me. "She just transferred to Hamilton. She's from the city. Near here, right?" he asked me.

"About forty blocks down," I said.

"Nice to meet you," she told me. "Especially since you look halfway normal and like you might have a brain in your head. Speaking of which . . . " She turned back to Baxter. "Did you go to that tutoring place?"

Baxter nodded. "Yeah, they can't help me," he said. "And they were expensive. Really expensive."

"Oh, honey. What are we gonna do?"

"I dunno. Can you tutor me?" he asked.

"If I could, I would," she said. "But if I'm going to keep my scholarship, I have to work around the clock as it is. You know that."

"Yeah, I figured," he said. He could barely look at her, he was so sad. Then he shook his head, like he was shaking off a fog in his brain. "Hey, I have stuff from Mom for you."

"Oh, boy!" Deb took the plastic bag from him and peeked inside. "Charmin, tampons, and homemade cookies. That'll get me through the weekend. Tell her thanks."

"Yeah."

"You want to come in? See the coven?"

"No, thanks. We're just going to drive around. Where's your—"

"She's over there."

We both looked up and saw a tall, angular girl with a cropped haircut standing uncertainly near the gates, smoking a cigarette and picking at her jeans. She gave a quick wave. Baxter waved back.

"Tell her, uh, hi," he said.

"I will. Thanks, doofus." Deb stood up on the footrest outside the door and gave her brother a loud, comforting smack on the forehead. "We'll figure it out," she said. "I'll talk to Mom and Dad."

"All right," he said. God, he looked like a giant little kid.

Deb waved and we drove away. "How come you didn't want to hang out there?" I asked.

"I wanted you to show me where you used to live, and whatnot," Baxter said.

"It's not because you feel weird about your sister's girlfriend?"

Baxter was silent. "That's a little weird. But no, I don't mind about that. She's a nice person."

I was quiet. Now the pieces *really* didn't fit together.

"Baxter, if your sister's a lesbian, and you're okay with that . . . why the hell were you bothering Pete that day?"

Baxter pulled the car over at a hydrant and put it in park. He looked at me, really looked at me, his face showing more frustration than I'd ever seen before.

"What?" I asked. "You're not going to attack me, are you? Because I already did that today."

"No!" he said. "Fiona, that wasn't what you thought it was. I wasn't bothering Pete. I was *protecting* him. That guy, Willie? He's crazy. He's dangerous. When we were kids, he used to shoot squirrels with a BB gun. I was keeping an eye on him, trying to calm him down and get him away from Pete. You totally misjudged the situation. I would never, never do anything like that."

"Oh."

"That's why I wanted you to meet Deb. I'm not like that. I've been trying to talk to you since you started school—you seemed interesting, and I missed my sister, and you remind me of her—but man, you just shut me down."

"Well."

"Don't you believe me?"

I thought about it. Replayed the scene in my head a few times. Yeah, it was possible that Baxter wasn't actively involved in Pete-bashing. And with the whole school situation . . . well, he seemed like a nice enough guy.

Then again, I'd almost gotten myself in deep doo-doo by trusting too soon.

"I believe you," I said. "I apologize." I'd trust

him, but I'd keep an eye on him, too. I wasn't a hundred percent sure about this. He was still a big doofy football player from New Jersey, no matter how smart and cool his sister was.

He seemed genuinely relieved to hear me say I was sorry, though.

"Look, why do you care so much?" I asked. "I mean, why do you want me to have this good opinion of you? Why would I stand out at all?"

"Like I said, you remind me of my sister," he answered. "Smart and . . . just different. Hey, you're not, uh—"

"No. As far as I know, I'm straight."

"Oh. Good. I mean, not that it's bad, but I'm glad you, uh—"

"It's okay." I patted his forearm. Boy, this guy needed some serious communication lessons. "Come on. Drive down a little. I'll show you where John Lennon used to live."

As we tootled around the Upper West Side, Baxter and I started just chatting about stuff. I told him a little about what it was like, the transition and everything. I guess the only person I'd spoken to about it was Pete, and that was always so jokey. Baxter was like a big boulder that I could talk to, and then when he said stuff, it was just a few words, but it made good sense.

I have to admit it: He surprised me.

"You know, you'd feel a lot better—a lot less stuck—if you had some wheels," he pointed out.

"Well, I do," I said. "My grandma still has my grandpa's old car. My mom has her own—she made my dad buy it for her as part of the divorce. So the Grandpa car is mine for the taking, if I can figure out how to drive it."

"You're kidding. What kind is it?"

"Um . . . red?"

"No, seriously."

"Seriously, I have no idea." I thought about it. "A Volvo?"

"You've got a Volvo? What year?"

"I don't know!" I sighed. "My grandpa died like seven years ago, but the car was older. He loved it." I paused. "It's a stick shift."

"I will teach you to drive that car," Baxter declared.

"What? I can't."

"If you can chase off Millman with that bulimia trick, you can drive a stick shift. I'm going to teach you to drive it."

"Um, okay."

"I just want one thing in return."

"Uh-oh."

"You've got to tutor me."

I looked at him. "Me? You've got to be kidding."

He shook his head. "You're in all the classes I need to take to get my academics up to speed. I used to get A's in those classes—I just need someone to help me out. Come on, Fiona."

"I barely understand calculus myself!" I said.

"Well, teaching it will get you to understand it better," he pointed out.

You see what I mean? The boulder speaks, and it speaks truth. And I did want to learn to drive—or at least prove to him that it was impossible.

"All right," I said. "It's a deal. But you have to apologize to Pete."

Baxter nodded. "Fair enough. I'm just not sure exactly how."

"I'll set it up. You, uh, kick it through the end zone."

He rolled his eyes. I'd obviously mangled my football terminology.

"Deal," he said.

We had to stick around in the city till after rush hour, so by the time we got back it was dark out, and chilly. I directed Baxter to my house and we sat out front for a minute.

"Is your mom going to be mad?" he asked.

"I don't think she'll even notice I was gone," I told him.

"Oh. Man." He shrugged.

"I'll see you in school tomorrow. And thanks," I said. "I don't know what I'd have done if you hadn't shown up."

He waved me off. "Find out what year that Volvo is," he told me. "If it's old enough, it'll still have the kind of engine you can work on, before they computerized the whole thing. Even if it's a later model and I can't figure out the electronics, at least I can show you how to top off the fluids and check the oil."

I hopped out of his little black tank and ran up to the front door. When I stepped inside, there was a weird smell. Something familiar. Oh! Cooking. Someone was cooking!

"Grandma?" I said, walking into the kitchen. Then I froze in place.

Mom was across the room, looking just as uncomfortable as I felt. Grandma was beaming, though. And at the stove? Mary Dolan.

"Isn't it wonderful of Mary to come over like this?" Grandma twittered. "Just like when you two were little girls. Fiona, sit down, we're just ready to eat dinner."

"Isn't it a little late for dinner?" I asked dubiously.

"Oh, it's a special night. Isn't this when sophisticated people eat, anyway? You and your mother should feel right at home."

Mary Dolan turned around, displaying the dish she'd been working so hard on.

"Sit down and enjoy. We're having sassy meat loaf. The secret ingredient is *salsa*!"

Wow. From Manhattan to sassy meat loaf in under an hour. Was my life great or what?

My mom plopped down in a chair heavily, like it was an effort just to be breathing the air in that kitchen. Mary Dolan brought her creation to the table. It looked like a big lump of sticky red meat-cake.

"A cow died for this?" my mom muttered.

"It looks lovely," Grandma said.

I just kept quiet. Mary's face was relentlessly cheerful. She was brimming with goodwill. My mom was radiating hostility. This was a recipe for disaster if ever I saw one. I was just waiting for all the brimming and radiating to set of a chain-reaction explosion of some kind.

Three . . . two . . . one . . .

"You're not eating," Mary pointed out.

"I'm not hungry," my mom said.

"Eat your meat loaf," my grandma ordered.

"Mom, it's really—"

"I'm not eating this." My mom cut me off and pushed her plate away. "I'm not sitting here and I'm not doing this. None of you people have any idea what I'm going through. God, you're all so small. Thinking about meat loaf when I've got things to deal with that you couldn't—"

"*Stop it!*" A high, thin shriek of a voice cut through my mother's rant, silencing her completely. I think it was more how weird the noise was than that someone was telling her to stop. We all looked around, in fact—and saw Mary Dolan standing where she'd just been sitting, but with her chair knocked backward behind her. Her little round face was red, her little blond pageboy was trembling, and her little hands were balled into fists. Whatever she was brimming with wasn't goodwill. And it was boiling over.

"You . . . are . . . so . . . selfish!" she squeaked. "God! I am so sick of you! You were such a bitch in high school, but I was still glad to have you back in town because I thought you'd have matured. But you didn't! You're still the same girl who stopped talking to me when you grew breasts and I didn't!"

"What the—"

"Shut up!" The shriek cut my mom dead again. "Ooh! You make me so mad. Your mother's husband, your own father, died—or didn't you notice? Not divorced. Died! And you were too busy with your city life and your city world to come out here and make sure she was okay!"

"I came out for the funeral," my mom pointed out. "And anyway, death is easier than what I've been—"

"Don't! Just don't!"

"You've got to stop doing that," my mom said.

"No, you stop! Stop, stop, stop! You have a beautiful daughter, your mom is so supportive of you, and it's nobody's fault but yours if you screwed up your marriage."

"Hey, that's—"

"I'm sorry." Suddenly the fight seemed to go out of Mary. Her shoulders slumped forward and she turned to my grandma. "Oh! I'm so sorry!"

"Sweetheart, calm down," Grandma said. "My goodness, let me get you a glass of water."

"No! No, I just . . . I'm sorry. The store isn't

working out. It's hemorrhaging money. I'm too stupid to even do that right. I know it looks . . . dorky. It's a dorky store and I'm a nerd and I did it all wrong."

"I think the store is lovely."

"Well, that's why I love ya, Bev." Mary sighed. "I think I have to go home."

"Please stay. Caitlin's sorry. Aren't you sorry, Caitlin?"

My mom just stared down at her sassy meat loaf.

"I am going to go home. I shouldn't have even come out tonight. I'm sorry, Bev. I'll see you soon."

Mary backed out the kitchen door like she couldn't wait to get away from us, and I couldn't blame her. My grandma glared at my mom, my mom glared at her plate, and I just sat there wondering what else could go wrong in the world.

Plenty, as it turned out.

chapter FIVE

I was nervous about going back to school on Tuesday. I didn't know if Millman would be all pissed off and weird about our little adventure at the mall. But he passed me in the hallway first thing, and gave me a friendly-but-distant wave, like nothing had ever happened. That was fine with me. I wanted to forget the whole thing and move on.

Besides, I had bigger problems, if you can believe it. I had told Pete the whole story on the way to school, and he was astounded.

"That disgusting pig!" he shrieked. He couldn't stop hugging me. "I shouldn't have left you alone with him—ever," he kept saying.

"I'm okay, though," I pointed out.

"But I'm soooo sorry. What if . . . Ugh, Fiona!" And he hugged me again.

Man, it was nice to have friends.

Then he astounded me. When I got to the second half of the story—my rescue and my trip to the city—it turned out he was actually willing to believe Baxter.

"Maybe it's true," he said. "Look, if I don't want to be judged, I'm sure not going to judge him. You know? If he says he was watching out for me, I'm willing to believe it."

See, that's why you have to love Pete. He's got

the kind of generosity that gives me hives. The world needs nice people like him.

The trouble arose when we were heading to our lockers and passed some big, colorful posters on the wall. They were typical, I was starting to realize, of this fishbowl world of reality TV: they were designed by an elite team of graphic designers, probably graduates of the School of Visual Arts or Pratt, carefully orchestrated so that they'd look remarkably like hand-printed signs drawn by ordinary high school kids. And here's what they said:

HOMECOMING HEARTACHE?
FIND YOUR IDEAL DATE!

This year's Hamilton High™ homecoming dance is going to be more than just a couple of punch bowls and a deejay. It's going to be your chance to find true love, or show off your stuff. Sign up in the student activities office for a team of experts to match you up with your soul mate—results to be announced at the dance—or participate in the all-student talent show, to be broadcast live from the Big Night. Sign up NOW to discover your soulmate and take your shot at stardom!

"Can they do that?" I asked.

"Do what?" Pete wanted to know.

"Copyright a public school's name?"

He shrugged.

"That's the lamest thing I've ever heard of. Don't people feel like they get enough attention on this show without adding this *Jerry Springer*-like circus in the middle of a school dance?" I asked, turning to Pete.

He was having a hard time looking me in the eye.

"Oh, no," I said. "Don't tell me."

"I signed up." He shrugged.

"For which part?"

He still wouldn't look at me. I grabbed him by both shoulders.

"For . . . which . . . part?"

"Both," he squeaked. "The talent show—and the matchmaking thing."

"Pete!" I dropped his shoulders and he started laughing and dusting himself off. But I was truly crazed. "What are you, kidding me?" I asked him. "You saw what they did to Claire. And to me, until I stopped them. Don't you see you can't control what they do to you?"

"I know! But—"

"But what?"

"I don't know! I thought it would be fun."

I groaned. "Oh, Pete, I wish you wouldn't. Millman's a snake, and I just want everyone to stay out of his way."

"Oh, you worry too much," Pete told me. "They'll match me up with some girl, and she'll be happy to find I'm a perfect gentleman. And who knows? Maybe Simon Cowell will show up and discover me. Right?"

I sighed and gave him a hug. "Whatever you want to do," I told him. "You know I'll be there for you."

"I was kind of hoping you'd be there *with* me."

"What, at the dance?" I pulled back. "No way."

"Way," he pleaded, shaking my shoulders. "What if they match me up with smelly Rhonda? Or what if they can't match me up at all? I need you there!"

"Oh, no, no, no!" I said. "What about my needs? I need to not be at a school dance in New Jersey being broadcast on a national TV show that's already made me look like an idiot!"

"Come oooon!" Pete slipped an arm around my shoulder and strolled down the hall with me. "You can make fun of people all you want. I'll even help you pick out a new Gunne Sax dress at JCPenney."

"You're evil," I told him. "Let me think it over. I'm promising nothing."

Just then I saw a familiar headful of bobbing curls coming my way. I gasped.

"Oh, shit," I muttered. "It's Claire. I haven't seen her since that episode aired. She's going to rip me a new one."

"I don't think so," Pete said. "I mean, I talked to her. She seemed to hear me. But she's kind of unpredictable."

Yeah. Unpredictable. Despite Pete's faith in his old friend, I expected a giant confrontation like the one she'd dropped on me after the episode I like to call "Fiona's a Giant Whore" aired. It wouldn't be smart, but Claire didn't seem capable of speaking without shrieking. And her temper—ugh. I was horribly aware that this could get ugly fast.

Pete knew it, too—and so did everyone around us. It was like one of those old Westerns. The hallway cleared out around me as people backed away, watching the two of us. I could feel the cameras turning toward me, toward her, focusing on the conflagration about to erupt. Everything seemed to move in slow motion.

She approached me. She looked briefly into my eyes. She dropped her notebook.

I couldn't just stand there. I bent to pick it up. She knelt down next to me and pushed a note into my hand. I looked at her, startled, and opened my mouth to say something. She silenced me with a barely perceptible head shake.

Then she stood. "Thanks," she said, and walked away.

"No prob," I answered, and stuck the note in my pocket. I looked at Pete. He shrugged. We stood there for a moment, self-conscious, as the cameramen kept the lenses pointed at us. They got some excellent footage of us looking around at nothing. Finally they backed away and went in search of more interesting subjects.

I breathed a sigh of relief. Pete had seen everything. "Come on," he said, dragging me to one of the camera dead spots. "What does it say?"

I unfolded the note. Claire's rounded handwriting jumped off the page.

One P.M. today
Second-floor girls' bathroom
Third stall in
MEET ME PLEASEPLEASEPLEASE!! Need to talk!

"Um, is she going to beat me up?" I asked him.

"I don't think so. I'll wait outside if you want," he said.

"You will?"

"Of course, best buddy," he said, looping that arm around my neck again. "Since you're going to come to the dance with me."

Note to self: Remember that Pete is unbelievably persuasive. Can get anyone to do anything.

Including self!

So have you ever sat around in a high school bathroom stall waiting to have a mysterious meeting? How about *any* bathroom stall? I'm guessing no. I had no idea how to handle this. Do I sit on the toilet? That's awkward. Do I just stand against the wall? Do I lock the door? What if someone else comes in? Not many people used this bathroom—it was sort of remote—and the production team hadn't been allowed to install cameras in any of the rest rooms. Whatever Claire had to say, she had to say in private.

Which was very refreshing, if a little nervous-making.

Finally I heard the door swish open. Claire appeared in the open stall doorway, held up a finger, and then walked past. I could hear her opening each stall door, and see her feet as she looked inside each one, making sure it was empty.

"Were you followed?" she asked me. I peered out the stall door and saw her standing on the garbage can, inspecting the fluorescent light in the ceiling.

"Uh, I don't think so," I said. "Except Pete came with me. He's outside."

"Yes. I saw. That's fine."

"Um . . . what are you doing?"

"Making sure this place isn't bugged." She jumped down from the trash can and went to the mirrors, eyeballing each one with the concentrated expression of a bomb-squad leader.

"It's not the Oval Office," I pointed out.

She turned to me, putting her hands on her hips. Her face was totally serious. I mean serious, like we really were in the Oval Office and about to discuss disarming North Korea.

"Just calm down," I said. "Nobody's listening. What's going on? Why am I here?"

She blew her cheeks out, then walked into the stall and latched the door behind her. Then she turned to me again.

"I have to tell you something," she said.

"I gathered that," I answered.

"I just want to . . . " She grimaced. Then she looked up at the ceiling. Then she twisted her fingers like she was trying to pull them off.

"Claire. It's okay! What's up?"

"I'm sorry." She looked up at me finally, meeting my eyes. "I apologize. I feel like a total, total, complete, undeniable, utter, massive basket case for freaking out at you like that." A tear escaped one eye, then the other, rolling down her face as she gazed at me. She looked exactly like one of those big-eyed, sad-animal paintings from the seventies.

"Oh, Claire, you really don't have to—"

"No! I do," she insisted. I saw that her hands were trembling.

"Claire, you're making more out of this than there really is, you know what I'm saying?" I said. "I mean, it's no big deal. It's okay."

"Just tell me you accept my apology."

Jeez. The girl took the term "drama queen" to a whole new level.

"I, uh . . . I mean, yeah, I accept, but it's not necessary. I mean, what happened to you next was way worse than anything you did to me."

"I know. I know, and it was totally deserved."

She sighed again, and leaned back against the stall door.

"Claire."

"Yeah?"

"You've never apologized for anything before, have you?"

She grimaced. "Not really."

I squeezed her arm. "You did a good job."

"I'm sorry."

"Stop apologizing!"

"Sorry!"

We both laughed. She seemed to relax a little. "I just . . . I don't know. . . . Whatever I'm feeling—anger, sadness—it overwhelms me and I can't hold it back. I've always been like that—it just gets me in endless trouble."

"At last!" I said.

"What?"

"The real Claire," I told her. "The girl Pete says he's been friends with forever. I knew you were in there somewhere, under all that . . . " I waved my hands around, indicating fireworks, or butterflies, or something else hectic.

She gave a snorting little laugh. "Well," she said. "I dunno."

"How about we leave this stall," I suggested, "and at least go sit by the sinks? We can talk this out without the Tidy Bowl man listening in."

She heaved another big sigh, her breath trembling slightly. "Okay. I feel better. I was so nervous about this."

"Hoo-doggy. No kidding," I said.

We unlatched the door and plopped ourselves on the sinks, which was the only place to sit without flushing—not exactly Camp David, but at least we weren't on camera.

"Look, I've been dealing with Joey for a year and a half now," Claire started to explain. "He's been my boyfriend forever, and he's been putting me through this crap for just as long. Before the show I could dismiss it all as gossip. But now that I've got photographic evidence . . . well, I mean, I can't deny it anymore. He's a player. And I've been played."

"It sucks," I told her. "It's the worst feeling in the world. But the only thing worse than getting treated that way is staying in the situation, you know?"

"I know! I dumped him. I mean, I'm trying to. He's acting all puppy doggy about it, but whenever I start to feel like taking him back, I think of all those pictures of him making out with other girls." Her eyes burned bright with tears.

"I'm really sorry," I told her. "If I'd known, I'd never have—"

"I believe you. I really do." She sniffled. I didn't know what else to do, so I gave her a little hug. She patted my back and sniffled a little more. It was weird, but . . . well, it was nice. I hadn't hung out with a girl since the beginning of the summer, and Giuli and Becky hadn't exactly been running out to New Jersey to see me.

"Are you okay?" I asked. "If you want to come over, or whatever, you can hang out with me and Pete whenever you want."

"I think I'll be doing that," she said. "I'm going to need all the friends I can get. This is going to be so hard!"

"Really sucky," I said. God, Baxter lost his college scholarship, Claire lost a boyfriend she'd been dating for most of high school, and Pete was trying to negotiate how, when, and whether to come out of the closet. My problems were beginning to look really small.

"I wonder if there's a way I could help," I said.

"What do you mean?"

"I mean, that guy Millman—he's the one who manipulates all the story lines, and I kind of have an in with him now. If I say something to him, maybe he'd lay off you in the next episode."

"Oh, I couldn't ask you to . . . Oh. Would you do that?" Claire actually clasped her hands together. She was so dramatic—but I was starting to see that every practiced gesture was like a piece of armor. Her overblown attitude was covering up her insecurity—an insecurity so deep she'd stayed with a scoundrelly boyfriend, locking herself into a relationship that was killing her rather than striking out on her own and facing the world single. Once I realized that, her little dramatic tics became sort of charming.

"I just don't want to go down in history as the biggest psycho in prime time," she added.

"Well, I don't think that'd happen anyway," I said. "I mean, there's always Ann Coulter."

"Who?"

"Never mind. Different reality TV. I'm going to go talk to him now. I want to get this over with."

"Should I come with you?"

"You don't have to."

"I want to. For moral support," she said.

"Oh, I can handle this."

"I know you can. That doesn't mean you don't need a friend along."

A friend? A friend. Huh. Who knew a trip to a bathroom stall could be so productive?

Another day, another knock on the big metal doors of the production office. Another glare from the chunky-glasses-wearing production assistant.

"You back for more?" she asked, with more than a hint of hostility.

"What's that supposed to mean?"

"Nothing. Hang on."

She opened the door wide. Mike Millman stood behind her with a broad smile on his face that I couldn't quite read. It wasn't like the distant smile I'd gotten that morning—not by a long shot. And it wasn't like the happy-to-see-me smile I'd gotten before our little ride to nowhere. No, this was some other kind of smile. . . .

I couldn't wonder about that now. I stepped inside his territory—the off-limits production office—and stood toe-to-toe with him. Claire stood just behind me. And I had to admit, now that I was here, I was glad she was with me. In fact, I wished Pete were there, too—but he'd had to leave for a doctor's appointment right after our big summit meeting.

"We need to talk," I said to Millman.

"No problem," he answered, seemingly undisturbed by the invasion. He led us into his office, a small cluttered room that must have housed the special-ed kids, since the walls were still plastered with big, cartoony alphabet letters, and he turned around, leaning back against his desk and crossing his arms across his chest.

"I want you to stop making Claire out to be the bad guy," I told him. "I appreciate that you did it to make me look good, because the first episode was such a disaster for me, but you went too far. You missed my point. I didn't want you to pick a different victim. I wanted you to stop picking victims at all."

"Hmm," he said, giving me a patronizingly fake serious nod.

"I'm serious," I insisted. "I'm not signing that release until I know you're doing right by me and by the students of this school."

"Release?" he asked, opening his eyes wide like this was the first he'd heard of it. Something was definitely not cool here.

"Yes, the release! You're supposed to get me to sign it before you air anything, and I can shut down production just by telling the executive producers I'm the only kid in this school not on board with you."

"Oh, right! Right, that release. I think I've got it over here somewhere. . . . " He started fiddling around on his desk.

"Don't bother!" I told him. "I'm not signing it. Not until after the third episode. I want to make sure you—"

"Here it is!" he said. "Are you sure you won't sign it? Because . . . oh, that's weird. My goodness, that is very strange indeed."

"What's strange?" I asked. "What's going on?"

"It seems this is already signed."

Claire gasped behind me. I reached out and snatched the paper away from him. There it was, in black and white—and turquoise blue, my mother's pen ink of choice. My mom had signed the form instead of me. Dated today.

"I—I don't understand," I stammered.

"No, I don't imagine you would. See, you're a minor. I never needed your signature—it was your mother or father who had to sign. Now, from everything you told me yesterday, I knew I wouldn't be able to get to your dad. But your mom? You gave me everything I needed to know about her. Depressed. Lethargic. Unlikely to ask questions. Oh, you were right. When I went to your house today, she was barely out of bed, and it was after eleven in the morning. She just sat there pounding coffee. Finally she signed just to get me the hell out of her house, I think. It was as easy as you said it would be."

I stared at him. "You little snake."

"Aaah, don't be like that," he told me. "It's just business."

"You scumbag. Mike, you can't do that. You went behind my back and—"

"And saved my show," he stated, finally dropping his faux-nice exterior and showing me his true, cold self. "I can't have some spoiled brat waltz in here and hold some piece of paper over my head. Not when my career's on the line. I play this show right, the next one is mine from the word 'go.' And you were getting in the way. I did what I had to do."

"Fiona, come on," Claire said, tugging my arm.

"No, wait," I snapped. "I'll have her retract it," I told him. "I'll have her come here and take it back."

"Sure, go ahead—but make sure you have a good lawyer with you. Oh, that's right—you've already spent every penny on lawyers. Well, that ruins that plan."

"I can't believe this."

"Listen, Fiona. Every show needs a Puck. You know what I'm saying?

"No, " I said. "I don't. Puck's a character from Shakespeare, and I'm sure that's not who you're referring to."

Millman sighed like I was the most annoying little schoolmarm he'd ever come across. "Puck. from the San Francisco season of *The Real World*. He was such a jerk that everyone in the house *and* in the audience hated him—and the show was a huge hit. Reality shows thrive on the Puck: someone who's so irritating, so useless, and such a major moron that everyone hates them. It might ruin that person's life, but the show . . . the show makes great ratings. And that's what really matters here, right?"

I was speechless. Yes, me, I was speechless. This I hadn't foreseen. Never mind the rug—the entire floor had been pulled out from under me. The earth had cracked. My mom had sold me out. And I was now at this guy's mercy.

"I'll tell someone about yesterday," I mumbled lamely.

"Go ahead. I gave you a ride and you misinterpreted it. I'm too important around here—they'll just tell me to be more careful. And I will be."

Claire tugged my arm again. "Come on," she urged me. "Forget about him. We'll figure this out. Come on."

If she hadn't been there, I think I just would have melted into the floor. Instead I let her lead me back out of the looking glass, into the normal-looking side of school.

Claire shook my arm. "Hey. You're shaking," she said.

It was true. I was trembling, something that had never happened to me before. I felt a level of anger and betrayal unlike anything else. My heart was beating a mile a minute.

"My mom signed that paper," I murmured. "It didn't even occur to me that she'd do that."

"Maybe there's something else going on. Don't freak out."

"And I sold you out for nothing." I turned to look at her. "I had one episode of looking good, and now we're both in trouble. I should have left everything alone."

"You did what you thought you had to do. You didn't know he was going to be such a jerk. You just made a mistake, Fiona. You're human!"

"But I . . . I thought I knew better."

Claire shook her head. "This thing is bigger than both of us. Bigger than all of us."

We plodded downstairs. The class bell rang, but I didn't hurry toward class. I headed for the front doors.

"Fiona!" Claire called after me. "Don't cut class! Come on, chill out; it's not worth it."

"I'll see you later," I told her. "I have to talk to someone."

"Who?"

"My mom."

When I got home, the house was quiet as a tomb. As usual. My grandma was out earning a living to put food on the table for the three of us, and Mom was downstairs in the basement feeling sorry for herself.

It was time for me to stop taking care of her. Obviously I couldn't fix her life. And the more I tried, the more I got screwed. Today it ended.

I stormed down the stairs and flicked on the light. The overhead light, not the nice little lamps we'd brought in. The room flickered into a fluorescent pale nightmare. Mom sat up on the bed, blinking at me.

"What the hell are you doing?" she asked. "Why are you home? Turn that light off!"

"What did you do to me?" I asked.

"What are you talking about?"

"You signed that release. A guy came here

today with a release for that stupid show and you signed it."

"Don't yell at me just because you forgot to have me sign one of your school papers!" she shouted accusingly. "You were supposed to take care of all that. It was your own responsibility; I just fixed what you screwed up."

"No, Mom!" I screamed. She jumped back, startled by my anger.

"It was *your* responsibility," I told her. "*You're* the mom. *You* were supposed to know what was going on with my school registration. *You* were supposed to watch out for me. That paper had nothing to do with my education or anything. It was my only safety net. It was the one thing I had that I could use to keep myself from getting manipulated and exploited by that stupid stinking show. And you signed it. You took my only lifesaver and tossed it to the sharks. Now I'm drowning, mom, and you're shoving my head under the water!"

"What do you—Don't talk that way! I'm your mother!"

"No, you are not!" I screamed. "You've never been my mother. I've been in charge all my life while you flaked on everything you ever had to do! You and Dad both! Well, I'm done! Maybe

Grandma will let you leech off of her for a while longer, but not me! I'm doing exactly what you've done for me: *nothing.*"

"Don't say that!"

"What did you do for me, Mom?"

"When you were sick . . . I sat up—"

"I was *five*!"

"Get out!" she shrieked. "I don't want to hear another word about your school or your show or any of it. Just get out!"

Uh-huh. I thought so. I shook my head, disgusted, and left the house. I didn't even know where to go. I just stumbled down the street till I got to a little park, then plopped myself on the bench. Then I pulled out my cell phone and dialed it.

It rang and rang. His voice mail picked up. And then I did something I'd never done before in my whole life.

"Daddy," I said. Then I burst into tears.

chapter SIX

I know! I know! I can't believe I got all girly and babyish! Look, I'm as shocked as the next person that it all got to me like that. But it did. I really didn't know where to turn or what to do. I am very used to having everything under control, including myself.

After I left a very boogery, blubbery message for my dad, asking him to call me ay-sap, I sat there for a while and cried some more. Not a pretty little sniffly affair, like at the mall. I mean I really cried, with big boo-hoos ripping themselves out of me. After a few minutes my head started pounding, and I actually felt like I was going to throw up. I forced myself to breathe in and out a few times, slowly. I wanted a bottle of water or something. I reached into my bag and found Baxter's bandanna from the day before.

"Oh, crap!" I yelled. I blew my nose and stood up. Then I started trudging back up toward my house. I was supposed to meet up with the big B for my first driving lesson after school, which by now it was. I didn't need my mom coming out of the house and, I don't know, signing my birth certificate over to him.

I should have been running, but crying makes you *tired*!

Anyway, he intercepted me before I could

even get there, pulling up in that little truck and beeping.

"Hey," I said, hoisting myself into the passenger seat.

"I was looking for you after school," he said. "Pete said you came home early. Were you crying again?"

"Never mind, just more family crap," I told him, tired of the endless complaints that were my life. If I was going to tell my mom to stop feeling sorry for herself, I had to take my own advice, too, you know?

"Wait a minute," I said, suddenly realizing what Baxter had said. "Did you say you talked to Pete?"

"I apologized. He was really cool about it. I feel like such a dick."

"Well." I shrugged.

"Claire was with him and she said you were upset," he went on, ignoring my kind-of-rude, I-don't-really-trust-you-yet response. "Something happened today with that guy? Did he try something funny again?"

"Millman? Nothing funny about him," I said. "But it's not like that. He just . . . Oh, God. It's a long story. Let's just say I'm still getting screwed by him—but just not physically."

I told him the whole sordid tale—how I thought I had one more ace up my sleeve, except my mom messed the whole thing up for me. I tried to tell it like a story, rather than sounding sorry for myself. Baxter listened, his face showing how angry and upset he was, but saying very little. Just letting me get it all off my chest.

"That's horrible," he said simply.

"Which part?"

"All of it. That he did that to you. That your mom did that. I can't imagine."

"It's sucky. But . . . I'm starting to realize everyone's got something going on."

"That doesn't mean your stuff doesn't suck."

"Thanks."

He sat there for a minute. We both just sort of stared out through the windshield.

"All right, come on," he said, driving the car over to a wide, empty parking lot behind the A & P.

"What? You're not serious," I said. "I can't drive in this condition."

"You can't drive anyway, so it doesn't matter what condition you're in," he told me. "Look, I've had to play football in every mood there is. You can't change anything this afternoon, so you may as well get something done. Shake it off. For now."

"I don't know."

"You're just nervous about driving. I know you don't want to sit around and feel sorry for yourself."

"No, I do not!" I agreed. "God! That's the last thing I want to . . . Okay! Fine." Baxter left the car running as we switched places. As I settled into the driver's seat, I asked, "What's this thing do?"

"That's the air conditioner. Turn it off."

"Um . . . "

"Hit the button again."

"I don't remember which button it was."

He sighed and hit the only button that was lit up on his dashboard. Then he looked at me with exaggerated patience.

"Okay, take your right foot and put it on that pedal on the floor in front of you," he said, and I looked down.

"This one?"

"Yes. Right foot. That's your brake. You push down on that pedal as you change gears." He showed me how to put the car into drive. "Now move your foot to the other pedal. That's your accelerator. The gas. Go easy on it."

"Okay."

"Now step on the brake. To the left. The wide one."

"Brake."

"Gas."

"Gas."

"Brake."

"Brake."

It was a weird little dance, but I thought I might be able to learn it.

The next morning—it was only Wednesday; can you believe how action-packed this week was?—I was at my locker when Baxter came up.

"Talk to you," he mumbled.

"What?"

"Need to talk," he muttered, eyeing the cameras warily. "Important. Private."

"I didn't do anything to your car, did I?"

He rolled his eyes. "Get Pete. Meet me . . . um. Where can we go?"

I looked at him, concerned, keeping my face out of the line of camera sight. "We can't exactly go to the girls' bathroom. There's that spot outside the gym—the one where . . . you know, where I first saw you. It's camera-free, as long as we stand in the right place. I'll get Pete, and we'll meet up right after first period."

"Now," he said, and stalked off.

Sheesh. I don't know how guys are supposed to talk to girls out in Jersey, but if this was the deal, I wasn't sure I was up to it.

I grabbed Pete, who was talking to Claire, and she came along, too. We were all too curious to hear what Baxter had to tell us.

"Maybe he's going to ask you out," Pete singsonged.

"Then why would he need you here?" I wanted to know.

"Nobody's dating my baby without my permission!" he shrieked in a diva voice.

"Right, you're straight." Claire snickered.

"I'm so glad I have a friend like you so I don't need enemies."

"Come on, there he is," I said in a hiss.

Baxter was standing alone in the hallway. It was weird seeing him there, where I'd seen him giving Pete a hard time—or, well, whatever was going on. Right now he had an uncomfortable look on his face, and his hands were stuffed in his pockets like he didn't know what to do with them otherwise. For such a big guy, he looked sort of small. It was strange, because he'd been so confident behind the wheel of the car, teaching me how to drive. And now there was this side of him.

"What's going on?" I asked.

"Something weird," he said. "I'm not sure where to start."

"Start with the gas pedal," I said, reassuringly, and he gave me a grateful smile.

"Okay. So last night I get home and that guy Willie calls me, from the team. You know, the one—"

"Oh, I remember him all right," Pete said.

"Yeah. Well, so he calls me because of that matchmaker thing for the homecoming dance. He said they were making a big deal out of fixing him up with someone, and he was calling everyone on the team to boast about it."

"Gross, imagine getting fixed up with him." Claire snorted. "I'd bring a straight razor on the date and tell him to lose the goatee before I got in the car."

"Oh, I thought you were going to cut his nuts off with it." Pete snickered.

"So what's so serious about that?" I asked him.

"It didn't sound right. I mean, I'm not . . . I mean, not that I notice or anything, but Willie's not exactly a lady-killer. Like Claire said. So I asked him if everyone on the team was getting the same treatment. And he said no. He thought I was jealous because of my leg. But really I was just trying to figure it out."

"And?"

"And he said that guy Mike Millman called him personally. Telling him all this stuff about how the show was going to do something *special* with him and his date. How he had to be ready for a real big surprise. He thought maybe they were going to bring in a porn star for him, like that time on *Howard Stern*."

"Oh, man," I said. "Millman's not a good sign."

"He's up to something," Claire agreed. "But what?"

"But this." Baxter pulled a crumpled piece of paper out of his pocket and handed it to me. Then he looked at Pete. "I'm really sorry, man," he said.

I uncrumpled the paper. It was a scribbled list of couples, like someone's notes from a meeting. I didn't recognize most of the names—but then at the bottom I saw some big block letters, circled three times and underlined.

They matched up Willie—with Pete.

"Oh, my God," I murmured. "They're going

to surprise Willie by giving him a male date."

"He'll go nuts," Baxter said. "The guy's sick in the head. He'll do something horrible."

"I won't go to the dance," Pete said. "Forget it; it's not worth it." He looked close to tears.

"I can't believe this," Claire said. "Pete, none of us will go. We'll take the train to the city that night. We'll have Fiona show us around."

"It's no big deal," Pete said. "It's just a dance."

"It is a big deal," Baxter countered. "This just shows how low Millman's willing to go. If he can't make trouble at the dance, he'll find something else to do. Someone else to hurt. This dance is just one opportunity—if he can't make trouble there, he'll just do something worse the next time. It's like my sister said, Fiona. If you let a guy get away with crap, he's going to hurt someone else. I think we need to figure out a way to stop him. *Really* stop him."

"Oh!" Claire looked at Baxter like he'd just turned into the Snuggles teddy bear. "Baxter, you're so amazing—like a knight in shining armor!"

"I'm serious," he said.

"I know you are. Baxter, where'd you get these notes?" I asked.

"I sneaked into the production office and stole them," he said.

"Oh, my God. You could have been caught on tape!"

"I guess."

I shook my head. Any shred of not quite trusting Baxter flew out the window. "You know what? You don't need me to tutor you, because you're obviously one billion times smarter than me. I bought Millman's bull from day one, and you saw through him. You knew he was behind this. I can't believe I was stupid enough to ever, ever believe him."

"Don't be so hard on yourself," Claire interrupted me.

But I was full of self-loathing. Here I'd been dismissing Baxter as a meathead, and thinking of myself as Miss Sophisticated. When really he had a mind that was ten thousand times calmer and more analytical than mine, and I was nothing but a flirty tease. Ugh!

"Look, everyone makes mistakes," Baxter said. "Right? I gave up on my schoolwork for football, Claire dated Joey—"

"Hey!" she interjected. Then she shrugged. "Yeah," she admitted.

"I never make mistakes," Pete announced.

"Okay, then you're the exception. The rest of us have to go through life knowing we might screw up. The important thing now is, we've got this information—and we can use it. But I don't think any of us can do it alone."

Man of few words speaks truth, part twelve.

Of course, what exactly we were going to do was still a mystery.

My phone vibrated in the middle of English class. I looked at it and saw my dad's number. Faking a coughing fit, I ran to the bathroom to answer it. No way I was going to miss out on one of his rare guest appearances in my life.

"Oh, my God, Fee, are you okay?"

"I am now."

"I talked to your mother. I really read her the riot act!"

"Oh, jeez, you didn't have to do that. There's no point anyway."

"Well, Fee, I mean, this is horrible. I can't believe she did that. I can't believe I didn't think of it as a possibility. I feel like this is all my fault." He paused. "She told me what you said."

"Well, look, I don't—"

"No, you were right, Fiona. We haven't done

right by you. I mean, parents have crises, but usually it's not both at the same time. I've been so distracted looking for an apartment and taking any freelance work that came along, and your mother—"

"It's a disease, I guess. Depression."

"You've deserved better. For what it's worth, I'm sorry."

"It's okay," I said automatically. And then he surprised me with another first.

"It's not okay," he told me. "You always say it is—but it's not."

I sat there quietly, not knowing how to respond.

"Anyway, I found some things out," he went on. "I got a new job—I was the sound man on an episode of *Law and Order*, and it looks good, like they're going to use me a lot."

"Dad! That's great!"

"Oh, yeah! It's good. I got you Jerry Orbach's autograph."

"Did you tell him 'nobody puts Baby in a corner?'" That's a quote from *Dirty Dancing*. Jerry Orbach played the— Oh, just see it. My dad and I watched it about five hundred times when I had mono.

"Uh, no," he told me. "But I did ask around

on the set to see if anyone knew this guy Millman. The guys didn't—but a couple of the girls did."

"A couple?"

"Seems he's got a girlfriend he lives with, but things aren't so good around the homestead. He's always running around on her, pissing her off, hitting on interns—and creeping people out because he's got a taste for—"

"The younger chickens," I said. "That's gross."

"If he lays so much as a finger on you," Dad told me, "if he gets close enough that you can even smell him, so help me, Fiona, I'll drive out there and—"

"Please don't. I need you employed and not in jail," I told him. "Besides, you know I can handle myself."

"I know. I know you can, hon, but it's my fault you're so damn good at it."

"Oh, look." I rolled my eyes. "Listen, thanks for the information about Millman. I think I can use that. And I'll let you know what happens, okay?"

"Call me every day," he said. "Tell me everything. Fee, even if I'm on set and I can't answer the phone, leave me voice mails. Long ones. I want to know."

"Okay, Dad."

"I'm serious. I love you, sweetheart."

"Jeez! Okay. It's okay. I love you too."

"Okay. I'll see you soon."

"All right. 'Bye."

I clicked off the line and blinked a few times. Okay, so he wasn't exactly running out to the suburbs to whisk me back to the city, but he obviously still cared. That was something. Maybe things were looking up.

Or maybe they were just getting weird. When I got home that afternoon, I was greeted with a truly bizarre sight.

Mom. Up. Out of bed. Dressed. In navy blue instead of black. Sitting in the kitchen.

With Mary Dolan.

"Oh! Uh . . . " I started to back out of the kitchen. If Mom was going to ask me to bail her out, I didn't want to hear it. I hadn't seen her since our fight—I'd slept upstairs on the living room couch, and only went to get my clothes in the morning when I could hear she was in the shower—and I didn't know what kind of ambush she had set up.

"Fiona," she said. "Come on in; come here."

"Hey, there," Mary Dolan said, giving me a sheepish wrinkle-nosed smile. "Sorry about my little fit the other night."

"Don't worry about it," I said. "Is everything okay?"

"Sort of," my mom said. "I mean, I hope so." She sat back in her chair and folded her arms across her chest. "Fiona, Mary was a good friend of mine a long time ago, and she's right—I dumped her for no good reason. I was just a snooty kid."

"Oh." Mary waved a hand in the air. "Well, sort of."

"And I grew up to be a snooty adult," my mom added.

Oh, no. It was revelation time. I wasn't sure I could handle two of these in one day.

She stood up. "I talked to your dad," she told me. "Directly. No lawyers."

"And you're getting back together and we're all going to live happily ever after?" I joked. Hey, when I'm uncomfortable, I joke.

"Uh, nooo," she said, giving a little laugh. "Actually, we still hate each other. But we both love you. So much."

"Oh. Ma, come on, uh . . . " I patted her back.

"No. I've been terrible. Just terrible. Fiona, it's

just that the world's been so black lately, and I forgot how to . . . how to live, or something."

"Well, it's okay," I said.

"Your father said you'd say that. It's not okay. Not for you, and not for Mary, and not for Grandma."

"You could have knocked me over with a feather when she came into the store today," Mary interjected. I've never been so glad to have someone say something perky. For real. I'd had enough heavy-mystery time for one day.

"She apologized right off the bat, and I just felt one million times better," Mary went on. "I mean, that's all I wanted. Just to know she understood how it felt. And then we got to chatting. . . . "

"The store's not bad," my mom said. "You've picked out some nice things. I just think you need better advertising, and a little bit of a change in how it looks."

"See, that's why your mom's so great," Mary told me. "When we were kids, she was, oh, like Martha Stewart, the way she could make a room look homey, or interesting, or pretty. Her locker! You should have seen it, she had a different theme every year."

"A themed locker," I said, giving my mom an

arch, amused look.

"One year the theme was *Rocky Horror*," she pointed out, defending herself.

"She really was interesting," Mary said. "Different. I thought she was great. The kind of fresh air we needed around here. And I was just asking her to come help me in the store."

"I'll sell the Passat your dad bought and invest it in the store," Mom said. "Mary'll make me a partner and we'll try to make it work together. She's so good at numbers, and I'll give the place a different spin—I think it could really work."

"You're selling your car? But then my car—"

"You mean Grandpa's car? I thought you didn't want it."

I sighed. Easy come, easy go. "No, that's cool, Mom. I think that's a way better use of the money anyway."

"How does the rest of the plan strike you?"

I looked at her. "I think you're out of bed," I said.

She laughed. "I don't expect you to forgive me right away. I've been a total jerk. But . . . look, I'm going to figure this out, okay? I'm going to try."

"Well, that's good, Mom." I tried to smile at her, but this was a shock. I was hoping she'd drop the navy-blue thing, anyway. The rest of it sounded okay.

"I'm going to borrow her right now," Mary said, standing behind Mom and squeezing her arms, giving her a little shake. "Hope you don't mind. We left you a snack—"

"It's pasta. Regular old pasta. I told her no casseroles."

"It's okay," I said. "It's cool. Go ahead."

They tripped out of the kitchen like they were the schoolgirls and I was the mom. Except . . . I don't know; it seemed kind of nice. I wasn't sure it would stick—it was a huge risk, going retail. But it was nice that my mom was making the effort.

I don't know. The world was just going topsy-turvy, was all.

And I still had to figure out what to do about Millman.

"I still have to figure out what to do about Millman," I complained to Baxter the next morning, when he picked me up to make me drive his truck to school. "I can't drive this thing. I'm too stressed out. Besides, my mom's taking my grandpa's car anyway."

"You still have to know how to drive," he said as he clipped the seat belt across my lap and jogged around to the passenger side. "And did it ever occur to you," he asked me, "that maybe you don't have to figure everything out by yourself?"

"What are you talking about?"

"I'm talking about me and Pete and Claire are going to meet up with you after school today. We're all going to figure it out. Together."

"Huh!" I put the truck in drive and we lurched forward. "So uh . . . really?"

"I mean, Fiona, what on earth are you used to? Don't you remember what we said about not taking Millman on alone? Didn't you have friends back home?"

I inched down the street, waving cars past me on the left as I hugged the dotted white line, terrified I'd hit the curb or scrape a parked car. "Well, sure I did," I said. "Sort of."

What was I used to? I was used to making dinner for myself because my mother had stormed into the bedroom after another argument with my father. I was used to talking my parents into going out to Jersey for Thanksgiving instead of just getting turkey roll from Zabar's. I was used to friends who were so busy being their own iconoclastic selves that there really wasn't much time for, oh, I don't know, meeting up to plan a simultaneous rescue-and-revenge plot. Suddenly we all looked a little shallow. Or, well, less than perfect, anyway. Maybe there was some room for improvement in my worldview.

"Well, that's good," I said. "That's good, then. Okay. We'll get together after school."

"All righty," said Baxter.

"Yep," I said.

We sat there for a moment. I was enjoying how nice the leaves looked, just starting to turn a little bit red.

"Fiona?"

"Hmm?"

"The light's green."

"Oh!" I tapped the gas and we moved, imperceptibly, toward school.

"How are you kids doing?" my mom asked when we trooped in that afternoon.

"Okay," I said. "Are you going over to that store?"

"I was there all day," she told me. She was wiping down the kitchen table, dropping the crumbs into the sink, basically acting like a normal person.

"Are, uh . . . how are you doing?" I asked her.

She stopped tidying for a second and turned to me. "It's okay," she said, her voice dropping low as my friends acted busy. "It's like . . . I mean, Mary had a good start. All I did was put things together a little differently, rearrange the layout, and put a fresh coat of paint over the wallpaper. We're talking about ordering some different stuff for the store—knickknacks and jewelry from some of those artists we used to go see on the Lower East Side. Nothing too crazy. Just, you know. Stuff."

She shrugged her shoulders. "I don't know. It's weird. Being with Mary is weird, but she's got a good heart, and that's been lacking in my life for a while now. I feel good, Fee. I think it's worth a try. If it doesn't work out, I'll find something else."

"Well. That's good, Mom."

"Yeah. I'm just so sorry about that release form. I should have—"

"Forget it," I told her. "It's done. And anyway, I should have filled you in on what was happening."

"I'm not sure I would have listened."

"So are you heading back to the store?"

"Oh, I have an appointment in town," she said.

"Not another lawyer . . . "

"No! No." She smiled a little sheepishly. "No, it's something else. You kids have fun."

And then she left the house. Left the house! For the second time in one day! Really, it was amazing.

But there was no time to marvel over small miracles. We had work to do. And if you think I'm going to tell you what we said, you've got another thing coming. If being on TV has taught me anything, it's how to build suspense.

chapter SEVEN

The night of the dance I was surprisingly nervous. I mean, a school dance—we really didn't do stuff like that at Stuyvesant. We went to clubs if we wanted to dress up and do the Watusi.

So that was a first. Getting dressed was an ordeal. I wanted to blend in, but not look like a dork—which, believe me, although I was settling into Hamilton a little more comfortably, still felt like two polar-opposite possibilities. I finally decided on a Betsey Johnson dress with an up-down hem, higher in front than in back, with a relatively subtle pattern of red roses on black stretch lace. The scoop-neck top made me look about ten times paler than usual, but it would have to do. Anyway, it fit pretty well, I had to admit.

Good ol' Betsey J. And good ol' Century 21, the off-price emporium near Stuyvesant.

Anyway, that wasn't the only worrisome event. In fact, the fact that I was going to my first school dance (*nerd alert! nerd alert!*) was sort of dwarfed by the fact that I was about to embark on possibly the most daring thing I'd ever done. If I was in this on my own, I don't think I could have done it at all. But knowing Claire, Pete, and Baxter had my back—and my sides, and my front, if need be—quieted the bumblebees in my stomach and made it possible to actually leave the bathroom and go downstairs.

"Oh, you look . . . Oh, my!" Mary Dolan snapped about twenty pictures as I tromped toward her, my stilettos thudding into the runner as I held on to the banister for support.

"Thanks," I said. "You're like the paparazzi."

"Can we sell stuff like that?" she asked my mom.

"Maybe not that, but there's a designer called Space Cowgirls that has some funky lingerie," my mom said. "Honey, you look like eight hundred thousand bucks."

"Not a million?" my grandmother asked.

"That's after taxes," I explained to her.

She shook her head. "I'll never understand you two," she groused. "It had to be black?" she asked me.

"There's red!" I pointed out.

"I see that. Well. You do look beautiful," she told me. "Like you're going to a very fashionable funeral."

"Grandma, you really know how to lay on the compliments."

"I know. Now who is this young man picking you up?"

"It's just Baxter," I told her. "We're going as *friends.*"

"I didn't ask," she said.

"But we are," I reiterated. "We're friends. Not boyfriend-girlfriend. Just regular friends."

"Mmm-hmm."

"Mom, tell her."

Mom gave me the same raised-eyebrow, pleasantly indulgent expression her mother was shooting my way.

"Mary?"

She blinded me with another picture.

"Forget it. It doesn't matter. Just make sure you watch the show," I said. "It's going out live—and I don't think they're going to be rebroadcasting this one."

We heard footsteps on the porch, and my grandma opened the door.

"Hello, not-boyfriend," she said.

"Grandma!" I hissed.

"Say cheese!" Mary said, and we were immortalized for posterity. For the record, I was glaring bug-eyed at my grandma, and Baxter was grinning nervously.

"I got you this," he mumbled, conking me on the arm with a plastic box.

"What is— Oh, no," I said. "Not— "

"A corsage!" My grandma positively melted. "Oh, well, I'd hate to see what he'd have brought if he were your *boyfriend*."

"Can we leave?" I snapped, shoving the cumbersome oversized lily onto my wrist. "We're going to be late."

"Tell her," Mary murmured to my mom.

"I don't know, she seems kind of—"

"Tell. Her."

"Tell me what?" I demanded. "Oh, boy. What happened now? Don't tell me Dad—"

"It's nothing bad," my mom said. "I just wanted to tell you when the moment was right. And, well, I guess there's no time like the present. . . ."

"Mom?"

"Yes. Well, your grandma and I—and Mary—well, we pulled some things together. And Mary knew someone who was a secretary in the admissions department, and your grandma helped me organize, and your father managed to fax a few things over, and, uh—"

"We got you into Trenton Academy," my grandma blurted out. "Full scholarship. You can start in January, for the new semester."

"You only have to stay at Hamilton High a few months longer," Mom said.

"Isn't that great?" Mary asked. "It's what you wanted!"

It was great. It was great! Great. This was exactly what I wanted—that is, if I couldn't go back to the city, I wanted to be at an elite prep school, where only the best were funneled into classes that honed their minds and pointed them straight toward the very best schools. Yes. Yes! That was what I wanted. . . .

So why was I avoiding looking at Baxter? Why did his presence next to me feel like a tar pit, a big, black, heavy thing?

"I can't believe you did all that," I told my mom. "I really . . . that's amazing. Thank you, Mom."

I was really touched. I was also just a little confused. Why wasn't I happy about this?

I couldn't think about it. I grabbed Baxter's arm—surprised, momentarily, at how thick his biceps were, even through his rented tux jacket—and looked up at him, not sure what I'd see.

He was smiling at me. Kind of sadly. But smiling. I don't know what I'd expected.

"We've got to get going," he said. I nodded, and we made our escape.

Out at the car, Baxter insisted I drive again.

"It's nighttime," I told him. "I've never driven

at night."

"Then you need the practice."

"I don't even have my learner's permit," I stalled. "What if we get pulled over?"

"I'll worry about it when it happens. Make like Ralph Kramden."

I sighed and pulled the car out into the street.

"I wonder what people are going to think," I said.

"About what?"

"About us showing up together." A nervous laugh escaped me. It sounded about as natural as Michael Jackson's nose. "They're going to think we're a real couple."

"Oh, yeah, they might," Baxter agreed.

I tried to look at him, but I was afraid to take my eyes off the road.

"Yeah."

"Then again, Claire and Pete are going together, too," Baxter pointed out. "They're not really a couple either."

"Oh. Yeah, so I guess it's not that weird," I said.

God. I sounded like an idiot. I did feel weird. Weird, nervous, confused, and basically completely off-kilter. Whatever kilter is, I was definitely off of it. Because the truth was, I felt nervous around Baxter the way you feel around a guy you like. But he was a football guy. He was the size of Bear Mountain. He was one hundred percent different from me. As I ran through all the reasons why I wasn't supposed to be into him, my stilettoed foot slipped off the gas and I hit the brakes. We lurched practically out of our seats.

"Oof," I said.

"All right," Baxter told me. "Come on; I'll drive. We do need to arrive sometime tonight."

How was it that he was so cool and collected? My insides felt like liquid. I just wanted this night to be over. If our plan didn't work out . . .

He started climbing over the parking brake, and I tried to slip across under him.

"Whoops," I said.

"Sorry," he mumbled.

All of a sudden we were face-to-face, halfway across. I felt his bulk, the warmth of him, the solidness, so close it was like we were two little electrons in the same atom. I felt frozen in place. I saw his eyes flicker down toward mine, and I didn't know what to do. I didn't know what he wanted me to do. I just . . . waited.

His eyes shifted away. "'Scuse me," he murmured, his breath tickling against my temple.

"Sorry," I peeped. We both slid into our seats, me on the passenger side, him behind the wheel. I was shocked to find myself feeling totally . . . well, devastated. I couldn't believe he hadn't kissed me. And I couldn't believe he'd *almost* kissed me. I couldn't believe . . . Oh, man. This whole night was one unbelievable event after another, and it hadn't even officially begun.

We drove the rest of the way to school in silence.

With all the pictures, bad driving, and almost-kissing, by the time we got to the dance they were an hour into the festivities. Pete and Claire rolled on us immediately.

"Where have you been?" Claire practically shrieked. "Oh, my God, we were so freaked out!"

"I told her everything was fine," Pete said.

"But you didn't know. Why wasn't your cell phone on?"

"You guys match," I pointed out.

"Well, so do you."

"No, he has a red bow tie. You have an entire matching ensemble."

It was true. Claire and Pete had pulled together

one of the most retarded and adorable things I'd ever seen. She was wearing an amazing gold lamé, off-the-shoulder, skintight number, and Pete's shirt was made of the same sparkly stuff. It could so easily have looked horrible, but it didn't. It was just campy enough to work.

Pete shrugged. "I just threw it together," he told me.

"You're really something."

"So are we ready?" Baxter asked.

"I am. You guys?"

"Sure."

We watched the stage, where the setups and talent show were going on. It was kind of insane. This was in the school gym, which was the size of an airplane hangar—just mind-bogglingly big to start with. At one end of the room the production company had constructed a stage that stood about six feet above the ground. I counted one, two, three camera guys on the floor, a couple on the stage, and two actually suspended from the ceiling. The was in addition to the usual cadre of black-T-shirted guys who followed us on a daily basis.

Behind the stage were three giant screens reaching from the floor of the stage almost to the ceiling. Sometimes they flashed a sort of light show, and sometimes they showed people on stage in various close-ups.

The floor was teeming with kids in all sorts of dress-up. That was kind of festive. The girls looked like exotic flowers, and the guys looked younger than usual in their ill-fitting jackets and pleated slacks.

The decorations . . . well, I don't know what usually happens to a high-school gym when dance time rolls around, but I have to say they hid the fact that this was where people usually played dodgeball pretty well. It looked nice. They'd found enough chiffon, in the school colors of purple and gold, to line the walls, and set up big, gothic candelabra that flickered with electric-lightbulb flames.

The overhead lights had been covered, and theatrical lights installed, giving the place a dim glow punctuated by spotlights from the camera crews. There was chiffon on the stage, too, creating two curtains between the huge projection screens, where the victims—I mean, talent-show contestants and matchmaking couples—were supposed to walk out.

When I peeked behind the chiffon—whoo! There was a whole city behind there of production assistants and extra camera people and who knows who else skittering back and forth in a kind of permanent panic. I could see that the main focus of the operation was behind and under the stage. That was probably where Millman was. Little did he know what was in store for him.

"Who's up?" I asked, peering at the stage.

"Looks like . . . yep, Judy Kreiger," Pete said. "Oh, my, doesn't she look scrumptious in that swimming-pool-green frock!"

"I didn't realize you could put that much lace on one dress," Claire added.

"Her shoes match," I pointed out.

"They're dyeables."

"They still make those?"

"Apparently."

Judy beamed, her blond hair sprayed and sculpted into a halo of stiff waves. A spray of baby's breath dotted her temple, and her nails were lacquered a shade of pink I can only describe as "kidney." But her face was pure Cinderella at the ball. So what do I know?

She peered expectantly across the stage at the narrow curtain in the other spotlight. We all peered expectantly at the same curtain. The emcee—I recognized his face from *Melrose Place* or some show like that—did the whole

"Who will it be? Who's her dream date? What's going to happen next?" thing. And then the curtain swished open.

Oh! Hello, Joey!

The crowd whooped. Judy looked delighted, which I guess was the only way she knew how to look after a day of primping and polishing. And Claire . . . well, I think she felt like she'd been punched in the stomach. I know I felt a little queasy. I took a look at her, and sure enough, she looked like she was about to blow a gasket.

I couldn't blame her. She'd dated him for a really long time, and it was hard enough having to see him around school without seeing him gallantly strutting across a stage to be paired with someone else in front of the entire student body—oh, yeah, and the entire world. Not to mention he was looking his absolute cutest. It must have been hard.

I saw her eyes widen, then turn bright with tears; her chest heaved a few times, like it was getting ready to split open. And her skin . . . A flush crept up her chest, then her neck, then turned her face bright red.

She was ready to blow. A hissy fit of major proportions was about to be let loose upon the homecoming dance population of Hamilton

High the likes of which hadn't been seen since Martha Washington discovered the state of the outhouse after the troops were done with it.

"Hey," I whispered to her, grabbing her hand. "Remember episode two. We've got bigger fish to fry."

She whipped her head around to glare at me, and for a second I thought it might spin all the way around and start spewing pea soup.

"Breathe," I told her.

The cameras swiveled toward us and stared, like they were curious aliens with one big eye each. Oh, they were hungry for that hissy. And Claire? She blinked once, then again. And the third time I saw the tears disappear. She gave a deep breath, then wrestled her mouth into a smile and managed to clap a few times, graciously, politely. I'm sure the only way she could manage that last touch was to imagine Joey's tiny head being squished between her clapping hands. But she did it.

"Good going!" I cheered under my breath as I joined her in clapping politely, smiling at Joey as if I'd never felt a thing for him. That schmuck. He gave Judy a kiss on the cheek, and offered her his arm. They walked down the little red carpet together, down onto the dance floor, and started dancing together as a trio of gorgeous black sophomore girls came out and did a wicked cover of that old En Vogue song "Never Gonna Get It," which I thought was both apropos and ironic in equal proportions. Like that's what every girl on the planet should be singing to Joey. And yet he was going to get plenty of it, that little operator.

Oh, well. The girls were amazing singers, and I thought they might have gotten some coaching or something. Which was fine. America didn't need a massive amateur hour to make fun of. I was tired of everyone taking potshots at us. I mean, at Hamilton High.

"Hey, are you ready?" a voice said behind us.

We turned around to see Haley, the cranky PA who had been giving me the hairy eyeball for the past few weeks every time I tried to get in to see Millman. It was funny to think how she'd annoyed me. Because now that she was on my side—and we had made sure, when we were planning this thing, that she would be on our side—I was really glad to know her. She knew what a creep Millman was. She couldn't do anything about it directly, or she'd lose her job. But she could sure look the other way while we borrowed some equipment. And if she let some information slip, well, she was a busy girl; she just couldn't help it.

Hey, you can't blame her. If Millman wanted a loyal staff, he should have been a nicer boss.

"All set for your your closing number?" she said to Claire.

"I'm ready," Claire said. "I'm good to go."

"You sure?" She turned to me. "You guys ready for everything?"

"We're ready," I said. "Thanks."

"Okay. Get your butts backstage. It's time for the last couple."

She gave us a nod and strode off, talking into her headset and a walkie-talkie phone simultaneously.

We headed backstage, listening carefully to the big setup. The guy from *Melrose Place*—or was it *Beverly Hills, 90210*?—was playing this up for all it was worth.

"The last couple of the evening," he practically sang into the microphone. "Who will they be? It's a pairing of magical proportions—and a surprise beyond anything you've ever seen! Who did our producers put together as the most romantic, perfect, *gooooorgeous* couple of the millennium? Who's the new twosome?" Oh, jeez, on and on he went, like his career depended on it—and maybe it did. It would have been funny if it weren't so sinister.

Millman was near us, in the dark backstage, which was teeming with activity. He was barking orders like he was General Dork commanding an army of headset-wearing megadrones, all moving in superfast motion.

"Is the little fruitcake where he's supposed to be?" he asked Haley.

"Everything's ready to go," she said noncommittally. "Mike, are you sure you want to do this?"

"What, are you kidding me?" he snapped.

"No, I'm not. I'm serious. I think this is a mistake. We could get sued—don't you remember that talk show, where the gay guy got killed because a straight guy was fixed up with him?"

"Of course I remember," he said coldly. "It was the only thing that put that stupid talk show on the map. Otherwise it would have gotten canceled years ago. The network doesn't care about lawsuits. They only care about ratings. And that's what I'm going to deliver: numbers—huge numbers."

"No matter what the human cost?"

"Oh, stop being such a baby," Millman spat.

I liked Haley. I liked her so much. She turned

to us, shrugged, and gave us the high sign. We were on.

By this time the emcee had brought Willie out onto the stage. He was dressed in a top hat and tails, only the back of the jacket had these big blue faux-graffiti letters embroidered on the back, spelling out *Hye Rolla*. He must have spent a thousand bucks on that stupid outfit. And he was prancing around like a massive tool, waving at the audience and proclaiming his status as a "big-time playa."

"I'm fulla class! I enjoy the finer things in life! I am the creeeeeam of the crop, y'all!"

Did I mention he was cheesy as hell? Oh, and slimy to boot?

We ran to the other side of the stage. Pete was there, looking queasy. "I thought you guys would never show up," he said.

"We're here," I assured him.

"They think I don't know what's happening," he said shakily. "They turned off the speakers over here. And I can't see. What if you guys weren't here?"

In Pete's big, scared eyes, I saw how truly evil Millman was.

"But we are here," I said. "We're totally here. Everything's going to be fine."

The relief on his face was worth every stomach cramp the whole ordeal had brought me.

Thanks to Haley, the speakers near us suddenly sputtered to life. We could hear the emcee finish up with his Willie introduction. He was laying it on so thick, I'm surprised anyone could even see the stage.

"And who's the lucky person who's going to share a night of romance with this fine, upstanding male citizen of Hamilton, New Jersey? Let's just find out—Willie, your date for the homecoming dance is . . . "

The curtain swished open.

Everyone looked up.

Especially Millman.

And out walked . . .

chapter EIGHT

Claire Marangello!

Oh, man, was it sweet. The audience didn't know a thing. They just let out a big whoop because of all the buildup, and because Claire looked hot as hell. And she just ate it up. For the first time in her life, she had every single eye on her—*every* single eye. She was the absolute center of cheering, clapping, yelling attention. She put her arms up in the air, RuPaul style, and gave a hip shimmy that would make a statue come to life. Then she strutted across the stage to Willie and had her Oscar moment.

She looked up at him adoringly. She took him by the arm. And then she planted a smooch on his lips that had to have made her want to gag. But she sold it one hundred percent.

And Willie? The guy was so full of Jack Daniel's at that point—plus the copious amounts of bull-hockey the emcee had been covering him with—plus the heady feeling of a whole crowd of people chanting his name, that he did the only thing a cheesy Jersey guy can do in a situation like that.

He ripped off his jacket, stripped off his shirt, and stage-dove into the crowd. *Hye Rolla* was written on his back, too, in permanent marker that was running with his sweat.

And then the music started for Claire's song. It was "Dancing in the Street," that old Motown hit by Martha Reeves and the Vandellas. (Yes, I'm also a music geek. It's one of the things my dad and I used to bond over.) It's an old song, but Claire had been rehearsing it like crazy, and it was so energetic and fun, I had to give her major props. The opening strains of the song came on: *baa-bup-bup-badaa-baaa, baa-bup-bup-badaa-baaa* . . .

"Calling out around the world, are you ready for a brand-new beat?" she asked the crowd, singing her heart out. Before too long another voice joined in and Claire answered, turning to welcome Pete to the stage.

"Up in New York City," Pete sang, winking at me in the wings.

Then they sang together, making that song sound like it was written just for the two of them. I'm telling you, you've never heard anything like it. My heart was just bursting with pride as I watched them and I realized they were . . . how do I say this without sounding corny as hell? They were more than my new best friends. They were the dearest people in the world to me. They knew me, my feelings, in a way my city friends never even bothered to try to do.

They had seen through my too-cool-for-this-school exterior and cared enough to help me.

But I had to tear myself away. I had a job to do.

As they rollicked through their song, I ran to the backstage area where Millman was. And if he was tense and yell-y before, oh, man, he was about to turn it up to eleven. Baxter was right behind me, holding the camera Haley had handed him. He didn't flick it on yet. He was waiting for my high sign.

I watched as Millman gaped out at the stage.

"What the hell happened?" he said. I nodded to Baxter, and he flicked the switch on his camera. Onstage, Claire and Pete's song was just finishing. The image behind them on the big screens . . . it wasn't of them anymore. Now it was of Mike Millman.

"What the hell is going on?" he asked again, turning around to face his staff. "Where the hell is the fruitcake? I thought we were going to set him up so Willie got matched with that little gay guy!"

"I don't know what happened, boss," one of the sound guys said.

Everyone heard the echo of their voices through the auditorium—and across the nation, via the simulcast—except Millman. He was too angry.

And now I was on. My nervousness vanished. I took a deep breath and stepped forward.

"It's not anyone's fault here," I said. "It's me. I set this up. I wasn't going to let you humiliate and exploit another student in this school. We deserve better than you and your exploitation, Millman."

He swung around and gave me the most vicious glare I've ever seen. How could I have ever thought he was hot? He didn't look like Matthew McConaughey. He looked more like Ted Bundy: blond, blue-eyed, and terrifying as hell. He exploded at me.

"You little bitch!" he shrieked. "Who the hell are you to interfere with my show? This is my show! And everyone in this school works for me!"

"They're just living their lives!" I shouted back. "And you turn them into plotlines. You use us, and when we're not interesting enough, you create problems—and destroy lives."

"Oh, my God, did you rehearse that in front of your bedroom mirror?" he said mockingly. "You pathetic little snot-nosed scrub. You come out here and think you're better than everyone. You don't love the kids in this school any more than

I do. You said so—in my car, when you were begging me to take you back to the city. And I would've, too, if you weren't such a baby about a little slap-and-tickle. What are you, going to stay a virgin forever?"

"After getting groped by you? I might," I said.

"I know! You little prude! You've got no sense of gratitude. I could have made you a star, but you had your *principles*, and your *friends*. But I've got ratings. And that's the only thing . . . "

Millman's voice trailed off. He'd finally noticed, through the fog of his fury, the echo dogging his every syllable. Something was up. Something was wrong. He turned, slowly, slowly, and looked through the now-open curtain (thank you, Haley) out into the auditorium.

And saw the back of his own head, out there on the big screens.

"What the . . . " he said.

"WHAT THE . . . " his voice echoed through the eighteen speakers set up around the room.

Remember that scene in *The Wizard of Oz?* The one where Toto opens the screen and Frank Morgan is standing with his back to everyone, working the machinery, spinning cranks and letting steam out and talking into a microphone? "Pay no attention to the man behind the curtain!" he thunders. But it's too late. Not even the Cowardly Lion believes he's anything but a funny little man.

Of course, the Wizard turned out to be a good guy after all. Millman was nothing but the Wicked Witch with leather upholstery instead of broom straw.

He turned to me, his eyes wide with horror, like he'd just been shot in the gut and was about to fall to the ground with a thud. Only he would have been better off dead. The color drained from his face. He aged about ten years while I watched. He broke into a sweat—no, it was more like a slow ooze of slime from his pores. And nothing came out of his mouth but a squeak.

He turned back to the open curtain. All faces were now turned toward him, not at the screen. A thousand little oval moon faces. And behind them? My face, on the screen. Baxter had come around to get my reaction.

And for the first time, I was perfectly happy to be on TV.

Baxter hit the button on his camera and the image flickered out on the big screens. Millman just stood there. Haley barked a few orders into her headset, and the music started up again; Claire and Pete were clapping, running up and down at the front of the stage, getting the audience riled up again so they could all dance the rest of the night away without caring whether the cameras were on or off. Baxter walked toward me.

"You can't go to that school," he said.

"What? You can't tell me what to do," I snapped, immediately defensive.

"Fine. I'm not telling you. I'm asking you. Stay here with us. Be on the stupid show. Tutor me. We can still get into good schools if we work like crazy. We need you here. I need you here."

It was the most he'd ever said at one time.

"You need me?" I squeaked.

Then he stepped forward and—

"Wait," I said.

"What?" he wanted to know.

"Your name. I mean, you're not just Baxter. You must have a first name, right?"

He rolled his eyes. "It's Dave."

"Dave. Dave Baxter. It's nice to meet you."

And then he leaned down, and—

Oh, why don't you mind your own business?

The Real Deal: Live Simulcast
Review in the Daily Post

Do you know, I actually had my column done early this week? I gave a nice, interesting preview of next season's hits, finished it on time, handed it in, and went home. But I work on a daily paper, and when news breaks, it's my duty as a journalist to leap into action and bring you the story as fast as I can.

Yes, even a TV reviewer. Middle East, schmiddle east, this is news.

Three words: What a show! *Last night's live episode of* The Real Deal: Hamilton High *shattered every preconception a television viewer might have. I have seen every show, from the littlest cable broadcast to the Super Bowl, for the last seven years, and I cannot tell you if this was scripted or for real. It was the most spellbinding TV I'd ever seen.*

By now, the bare facts are known to everyone on the planet. The show's director, Mike Millman, was caught on-screen trying to humiliate a gay member of the student body by fixing him up with a homophobic musclehead. When he was found out, he lost his temper and admitted to all sorts of dirty dealings, including an R. Kelly-style flirtation with off-limits jailbait. Which means the end of his career.

Last night we just thought that. But as I was burning the midnight oil to file this story, I received a call from a source inside the industry—a sound man from Law and Order, *if you must know—who told me the word on the street is that Millman's been canned, fired, reassigned to the unemployment line. And named in a lawsuit by the network. He stands to lose everything.*

I guess every show needs a Puck. Millman certainly fits the bill.

I have to admit, though, there's a part of me—and I'm not proud of this—that's disappointed. Okay, so the guy was an evil slimeball. But that was some great entertainment! I've become totally invested in the lives of these kids. Will I still get to see what happens to them? Who was the "fruitcake" Millman was going to set up? What plotlines will emerge now that he's not playing puppetmaster?

I guess only time—and the rest of the season—will tell.

Oh, and did I mention the fantastic finale? Turns out Pete and Claire have more than just dramatic lives to trade on. When the students lapsed into silence, unsure what to do, it could have been a riot of Carrie*-like proportions. But Claire came out for her closing number, and she was joined by Pete in a last-minute switcheroo. They're like Sonny and Cher—funny, sweet, and fantastically talented. I smell spin-off!*

And of course, I've saved the best for last. It looks like Fiona—the original main character, the girl who got played by Joey with humiliating results in the first few episodes—has found herself a whole new plate o' fries. Maybe I'm mistaken, but I did freeze-frame it on the TiVo a few times, and I swear I saw her and Baxter, a football star who's been sidelined by a bum knee, move in tight for a long, lingering smooch. Could this mean love for the city girl relocated to the 'burbs?

Oh, you can bet I'll stay tuned to find out!

They Wear WHAT Under Their Kilts?

by Katie Maxwell

Subject: Emily's Glossary for People Who Haven't Been to Scotland
From: Mrs.Legolas@kiltnet.com
To: Dru@seattlegrrl.com

Faffing about: running around doing nothing. In other words, spending a month supposedly doing work experience on a Scottish sheep farm, but really spending days on Kilt Watch at the nearest castle.

Schottie: Scottish Hottie, also known as Ruaraidh.

Mad schnoogles: the British way of saying big smoochy kisses. Will admit it sounds v. smart to say it that way.

Bunch of yobbos: a group of mindless idiots. In Scotland, can also mean sheep.

Stooshie: uproar, as in, "If Holly thinks she can take Ruaraidh from me without causing a stooshie, she's out of her mind!"

Sheep dip: not an appetizer.

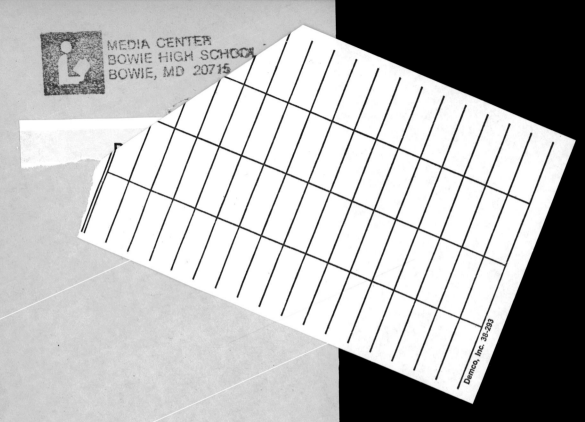